Twisted

A Twisted Fairy Tale

Lena Mae Hill

Table of Contents

Chapter One

Cayenne

Already anticipating my visit to Granny, I was tempted to throw her apples into the basket and rush out the door. But Granny Golden would tell me to take my time, that care could be taken with every task, no matter how small. Stilling my impatience, I arranged the apples in my basket, shining each one before nestling it into place with the others.

"Red delicious," said one of my dads, leaning over to snag one. "My mother's favorite."

"Wash your own apples." I slapped his hand away, rolling my eyes when he hopped around shaking his fingers as if I'd broken them. "These are for Granny."

"You're not missing out," Malik said to Dad. "Haven't you ever wondered why Cayenne's apples are shinier than anyone else's? The secret's in the spit."

"Caye's apples?" said one of my sisters, popping her curly ginger head into the room. Like me, my sisters had all inherited Mom's redheaded gene.

"Ah, the old spit shine," Dad said. "A classic."

"Y'all are gross," I said as I surveyed my tidy basket to make sure it would meet Granny's standards. "I would never spit on Granny's Golden's food."

I bumped another one of my sisters out of the way with my hip when she reached for an apple. We had to call our grandmas by two names so everyone would know which one we meant. With five dads, things could get complicated. Like most witches, Mom had a collective of husbands.

"Be careful," she warned, swinging my velvet cloak around my shoulders.

"Mom, I'm fine," I said, trying to pull away. "No one is going to kidnap me and steal my magic."

Mom held tight to my cloak and made me look at her. "That's not funny," she said quietly. "That happened to a lot of witch children when your father was growing up."

"I know, and if it had happened to him, I wouldn't be here today," I recited with a sigh. "I know. I'll be careful. But no one steals witch children anymore, and I'm not a child."

"And she'll kick their ass with her superior magic if they try," Malik said, hopping down from the stool at the counter and grabbing an unpolished apple from the box. As my intended, he knew better than to steal my apples. He tossed apples to my two hovering sisters before biting into his own.

"There are still goblins in the valley," Mom said, but Malik had already slipped between us.

He grabbed the handle of the basket and slid an arm around me. "I'll walk her up the mountain."

I rolled my eyes, but I didn't pull away from his familiar embrace. "As if you could protect me," I said. "I could suck up your magic in one gulp."

"Don't even joke about that," Mom said with a frown.

"Like a frog snapping up a fly," Malik agreed with an easy grin, sticking out his tongue to demonstrate.

"Don't be such a worrywart, Mom," I said lightly, stepping over to give her a quick kiss on the cheek. "I can protect myself from anything out there. Witches, werewolves, and goblins included."

"Yeah, goblins only steal girls to sing for their king, and no offense, but have you heard your daughters sing?" Malik asked.

He winked at Yarrow, who ran away giggling.

"Hey," I protested, giving his ribs a hard poke. It was true, though, so I didn't summon a rock out of the ground to stub his toe as we left the house. He was, after all, putting my parents' minds at ease. Though they worried incessantly over their children after living through the dark period of my grandfather's evil, I'd never known anything but our peaceful little coven in the First Valley.

Sure, sometimes parents argued, sisters punched each other, and friends hurt each other's feelings. But that was just part of life. For the most part, we all got along whether we were witches, faeries, elves, or dwarves. We grew our food and tended our gardens, learned magic, and cared for our animal familiars. We helped our neighbors, obeyed our parents, and were patient with our younger siblings.

Frankly, it was really freaking boring.

"Want me to walk you all the way?" Malik asked as we huddled together against the stinging wind.

"I think I know the way to Grandma Golden's," I said, shaking my head.

"I know you do," Malik said. "I just wanted an excuse to spend more time cuddled up with you."

"Aww, you don't need an excuse for that," I said. "My parents are practically begging me to officially add you to my collective."

"You did choose me as your intended a year ago," Malik reminded me.

"I know," I said, drawing away from him a bit. I didn't know exactly why I hadn't gone through with making it official. Witches could add as many people to their collective as they wanted, so it wasn't like I could never choose anyone else. And either of us could end the arrangement if it wasn't working anymore. There was literally no reason to stall the ceremony.

As we walked, Malik waved at the other witches we passed and greeted them all by name like the perfect boy that he was. Sometimes he made me feel…really crappy, actually.

I just wasn't naturally as *good* as Malik. I wanted things I couldn't have. I wanted more than the Winslow Coven and the First Valley. I'd never even set foot in the Second Valley, where the werewolves lived, and rarely went to the Third Valley, where shifters lived.

"Where are you off to this evening?" asked Yvonne, a busy-body who everyone our age tried to avoid. She was always butting into our conversations, acting like she belonged with our generation instead of our parents', which was super awkward. She even used beautifying spells to make herself look young like us and wore the same clothes as us.

Of course Malik was the one person who had a kind word and a smile for even the coven's least popular member. If we'd ignored her, she probably would have walked off in a huff, but Malik greeted her as he did everyone else.

"So where are you going this late?" she asked again, fluffing her blonde hair as if to make sure we noticed its suspiciously glossy shine.

"Just visiting Grandma Golden," I said, holding up the basket of apples as an explanation. My familiar, a robin named Robin—because what else would he be named?— nestled among the fruit.

"Oh, how's she doing?" Yvonne asked, joining us on the path.

I rolled my eyes over Yvonne's head. Our moms always told us to be kind to her, so we humored her, but I wished she'd just go away.

"She's been a little slow this winter," I said. "I try to visit every week to help her with chores."

"They say her mind comes and goes," Yvonne said, biting at her plump red lips. "Such a shame."

"Yeah, I really better get to her house," I said. "In case she needs me."

"Be careful," Yvonne called out, stopping at the well and letting us continue on without her. "It's getting late, and you never know what's lurking in the dark."

"What a weirdo," I muttered as we hurried out of Yvonne's earshot.

"She's harmless," Malik said, taking my hand. "Now, where were we? Oh, yeah, we were talking about how you shouldn't wait too long to start your collective, because some other witch might steal me away. I have to go with the one who's going to protect me the best."

I laughed and rolled my eyes again. "Right. In that case, you'll never ditch me for another witch because I'm obviously the best protection you could get."

"Hmm, true," he said with a dismissive shrug. "Guess I won't leave you just yet."

"You better not," I said. "But you can leave me here and go back home. You know my parents are paranoid over nothing."

"All our parents are paranoid," he said. "They went through the bad old days."

Granny's husband had been the Most-Powerful-Warlock-in-the-World, a man whose power had gone to his head, turning him evil. I'd heard all the cautionary tales about how I had to reign in my own magic and do cleansing ceremonies when I had mean feelings, and blah blah blah.

Basically, it didn't affect me, except that I got to hear Granny's wild tales of how one of her other husbands betrayed her, went rogue, and stole entire covens to suck out their magic and leave them empty, like Granny.

I turned to face Malik on the path. "Can you imagine, back then they couldn't even start a collective until they'd finished school and learned to control all the elements."

"It was important that they could defend themselves and their families before they started bringing more children into the world."

I stood on tiptoes and gave him a soft kiss on the cheek. "Yeah, so just be happy you don't have to wait that long."

"Oh, I am," he said, tugging my hood over my pepper-colored hair. Most people thought that's where I got my name, but it was only partly true. Mom had also honored our bit of fae heritage by naming me after a plant, as was fae tradition.

Malik pulled me close, and I lay my head on his shoulder and held him for a moment. For as long as I could remember, we had been intended for each other—long before I'd said it out loud. Our parents were close friends, and we'd played together since we were kids, almost as if we all belonged to the same big family. It hadn't been until a few years ago that I'd noticed, when my little sister pointed it out, that Malik was also hot.

Besides that, he'd always looked out for me, he had a strong capacity for magic, and he'd die for me if it ever came to that. Overall, he was a logical choice for my collective. There had never been any doubt in my mind—or the mind of literally anyone in the coven—that he would be the first I added. That was probably the real reason I hadn't. I loved Malik, and rationally, I knew he'd be a great husband.

For once, I wanted something unexpected to happen, something as exciting as Granny's stories about breaking tradition and marrying a fae or being kidnapped by pirates. She had an endless supply of stories from her youth, stories full of passion, adventure, and danger. Since I had none of that, I contented myself with visiting her and putting off my safe, logical marriage.

When I pulled away, Malik tucked my red cloak around my cheeks. "Stay warm, Cayenne," he said. "See you tomorrow at the eclipse."

Chapter Two

Cayenne

I followed the trail up the mountain until I came to the old rock wall that separated wolf territory from our territory in the First Valley. Mom had warned me time and again not to cross into wolf territory. According to several of my dads, wolves instinctually distrusted witches and just about everyone else. Plus, they were in a bloody turf war with the shifter clan in the Third Valley. Thankfully, neither side had come to us seeking magical interference...yet.

I needed willow bark for Grandma Golden's various aches and pains, though I never quite knew which were physical and which were the result of her experiences with her crazy ex. Unfortunately, the willow tree was on the very top of the mountain next to the lighthouse, and though I didn't have to step into wolf territory, I had to follow the border wall to find it.

Trailing along the flat plateau of the mountaintop where the wall ran, I pulled my cloak around my shoulders. Wind whipped at me, the grey sky only encouraging the brutal, barren cold of February. When I reached the clearing around the sealed lighthouse that topped the mountain, I scanned the surrounding woods. The willow grew at the edge of the clearing, and soon I spotted it. I peeled off a few strips of bark and tucked them into my basket with Robin and the apples.

Turning to go, I peered up at the lighthouse, an odd addition to an Ozark mountaintop. There were tons of stories about how it had gotten there, when and how the doors had been sealed, and what had happened inside it. Though I didn't believe most of them, the building always gave me the creeps. It stood sentinel over the valleys, a blank white tower that reminded me of a blind, unseeing eye watching over us. After giving it one last glance over my shoulder, I hurried back into the woods. They provided comfort, somehow, although I could still see the tower through their bare, leafless branches.

I was twisting around to crane my neck at the tower when hands clamped down on my shoulders. With a cry of surprise, I turned to face forward, my heart slamming. I'd walked right into a freaking giant!

"Better watch where you're going, Little Red," his gravelly voice chided. "You might fall and hurt yourself."

A teasing smile played across his lips. For a moment, I was captivated by his eyes, a warm green sprinkled with flecks of gold. He wasn't a literal giant, but he may as well have been. He stood a good two heads taller than me, with shoulders at least twice as wide, and washboard abs that tapered to narrow hips. I could see his muscles right through his thin white T-shirt.

"Oh, I don't think that's going to happen," I said, recovering myself and lifting my chin to meet his eyes. "I have a knack for working with my surroundings."

"You're a witch."

"And you're in our territory."

He hesitated, then nodded. "I guess I am."

I pulled my gaze from his. The intensity of his eyes unnerved me, which was something that didn't happen often. My thoughts turned to Malik, and I felt guilty somehow, as if I'd insulted him by thinking he couldn't unnerve me.

He never has...

This guy, however, kept studying me, drinking me in with his eyes as if memorizing every freckle on my nose, every curl in my cayenne-colored hair. His own hair was a mess of wild, bristling tufts, and his arms were covered with tattoos from the back of his hands to where they disappeared under the straining sleeves of his T-shirt.

"And... What did you come here for?" I asked. "Can I help you?"

"I came here for you, naturally," he said, a smile twisting the very corners of his lips again.

"Me?" I took a step back, instantly defensive. My mother hadn't told me all those stories about kidnap for nothing. Sure, they were annoying, but I must have internalized some of them. My heartbeat picked up speed despite my confidence in my strength, and my familiar flapped his wings in agitation.

"Yes you, Little Red," the man said with an arrogant smirk.

"What do you need from me?"

"It's more what you need from me." His face turned serious, his eyes sympathetic. "I'm afraid I come bearing some bad news."

I tried to quell my impatience, putting my hand on one hip. "Well? What is it?"

"It's your grandmother."

Something inside my chest lurched. "Grandma Golden?"

He didn't have to answer. The sympathy in his eyes said it all.

"I'm just going to see her now," I said, as if that fact alone would protect my grandmother, whose magic had been stripped before I was born. She had no protection of her own and was spacy on her best days. I couldn't imagine how that felt—to be completely helpless, dependent on the skills and tools of an ordinary human.

"I'm sorry," the man said.

"What happened?" I said, transferring the basket from one hand to the other.

"She's been taken," he said. "By the wolves."

My breath caught. My mother was always warning me to stay out of the other valleys, to avoid both the wolves and shifters until they had worked out their problems and stopped fighting with each other.

"What? Why?"

The man shrugged.

"I have to go," I said, stepping off the path, onto the leaves. "I have to see for myself."

"I'm really sorry," he said, following me as I hurried along the path. "If there's anything I can do…"

"You've done enough," I snapped. It wasn't fair to shoot the messenger, but I wished he'd just go away. I rushed along the path, all the way along the ridgeline and through the barren trees, until I reached the rock wall that marked the boundary. When I turned around at last, the man was still there, walking ten paces behind me with his hands shoved into his pockets.

Without a word, I turned down the mountain and forged ahead, deeper into the First Valley. Grandma Golden lived at the far end of the valley, alone in her drafty little cottage. My father was always trying to persuade her to move closer to the coven, but so far, his efforts had been wasted. Now, as the evening drew closer, I cursed my grandmother's stubbornness, her eccentricities, and her refusal to move closer to her family.

It was full dark before I turned down the path towards the small, secluded cottage. The wind shrieked through the bare branches, and I pulled my cloak shut around myself. Somewhere behind me, a branch snapped, and I spun around, my heart pounding.

You're being ridiculous, I scolded myself. *Are you going to be afraid of the dark next?*

Still, I held out my hand, palm up, and called forth a small flame. It flickered out in a gust of wind, and I had to use a ball of fire instead, which took more magic. My coven was very careful of wasting magic, always warning the young witches not to use it for their own convenience. But I thought this counted as safety, not convenience. Convenience would have been carrying a fireball to warm my hands as I walked.

I could make out nothing unusual on the shadowy path behind me. The sky remained a deep, navy blue in the west, but all I could see were the skeletal fingers of tree branches reaching for it. Some of the trees, I knew, contained ghosts who had tried to haunt human victims after dying. The trees had never bothered me, though. I could have had them bowing at my feet if I wanted.

Again, that was considered a waste of my magic, so I never had. But they didn't frighten me. It was the snapping limb that had me spooked.

I turned forwards and hurried on, almost running. Yes, I was being ridiculous. Knowing it did little to calm my nerves, though. What had happened to my grandmother? If she'd been all the way out here, how could the wolves have taken her? They would've had to come into the First Valley the same way I had and crossed to the very end before reaching her cottage. Surely they wouldn't be reckless enough to do that. And if they were willing to risk that just to kidnap a crazy old lady who lived in the woods, they must've had a reason.

But why?

I was still turning it over in my mind when the cottage came into view. I breathed a sigh of relief and slowed my pace. There was nothing in the woods. I was perfectly safe. Still, when I heard a rustle in the leaves to my left, I turned and shot a fireball at it. The dry leaves burst into flames in the spot I'd hit. After a moment, they sputtered out, leaving only a glowing orange outline where they'd scorched the leaves. I waited another moment to make sure they'd gone out before I turned back to the cottage.

Hurrying on, I refused to be distracted, even when I heard a twig snap followed by a painful silence, as if someone had frozen when they'd made a sound. I would not even dignify my fear with a response. A little magic could take care of anything in those woods. I marched straight up the steps of the stone cottage and threw open the door.

Inside, darkness swallowed me completely. Holding out my hand again, I lit a small flame. This might count as convenience, but I wasn't going to worry about it. I was too busy worrying about Granny Golden.

The cottage, usually toasty and full of some wonderful aroma, stood silent and as cold as the night outside. No welcoming scent greeted me—not baking bread, drying herbs, or apple sauce bubbling on the stove. How long had it been since I'd visited my grandmother? A week? Ten days? The cottage felt as empty as if it had been unoccupied for years.

Calling Granny's name, I hurried to the bedroom and felt for the light switch, flicking it up and down several times before giving up. The electricity was off. This in itself wasn't so unusual. Granny Golden constantly forgot little things like paying her electric bill. But combined with the cold and empty house, it only made the abandonment more complete. It made Granny Golden's disappearance real and urgent.

I shivered and crossed my arms, hugging myself as if it could hold back the ache in my throat, the pressure behind my eyes. I would not cry. That would mean she was gone.

"I'm going to find you," I whispered to the empty bedroom. "I promise."

I found a candle on the nightstand and pinched the wick between my fingers, igniting it. The tiny flame sputtered and then swelled, its light flickering off the walls and the handmade quilt covering the neatly made bed. How many times had I lain on that quilt, listening to my grandmother tell stories about growing up as a witch in the sixties? How many times had I fallen asleep here because I'd been so caught up in learning some new potion or herbal remedy that I'd forgotten to start for home until dark?

At least my parents wouldn't worry. They'd assume I was staying with my grandmother, something they always encouraged. Like most parents, they didn't think I could get into much trouble staying with an aging, magic-stripped witch. I had until the eclipse the next night to hunt down my grandma and get her back. If I didn't show up to the eclipse celebration with Granny in tow, my parents would definitely start worrying.

So I'd better find her quick.

With that thought, I pulled my cloak tight around my shoulders and stepped out onto the porch. I fell back against the door, stifling a scream, as a shadow loomed over me.

Chapter Three

Cayenne

"It's me again," a deep, gravelly voice growled out of the darkness. "Don't light me on fire."

Producing a flame, I could make out the muscular form of the man from the mountain. Closing my hand around the flame, I snuffed it out. I didn't want him to see my shaking fingers and know how much he'd scared me.

"What the hell?" I said. "You can't just jump out of the dark at someone."

"Sorry," he said, not sounding at all sorry. If anything, he sounded like he was trying not to laugh.

"What are you doing here?" I demanded, my back still flat against the door.

"I wanted to make sure you were okay," he said. "You seemed upset when you stormed off the mountain."

"You'd just told me my grandmother had been abducted. So, yeah, it's safe to say I was a teeny bit upset."

"That's why I came to make sure you were okay."

"Then I'm sorry to disappoint you, but I'm not okay. You're right. She's gone. It looks like she's been gone for a while."

"I don't know how long," he said. "But I know where she is."

"Who are you?" I asked, pushing away from the door to glare up at him. "How did you even know where I lived? Why are you the one telling me this? And how do you know my grandmother?"

"I know who has your grandmother because I'm… a wolf. Sometimes."

I swallowed hard, my eyes scanning him again, as if he might have some outward tell. But werewolves didn't look any different than normal people—until the full moon.

"Then why would you tell me?" I asked, my eyes narrowing.

"Because it's sick to hurt an old woman."

"You're betraying your own people to tell a total stranger about it, out of the goodness of your heart?"

He cracked a smile. "I'm not really one of them. I'm a shifter. I can be a wolf when I want. I was a member of a pack for a while, but when they found out I wasn't a 'real wolf,' I was shunned."

I narrowed my eyes at him. "What are you really?"

"I told you, I'm a shifter. I can be a wolf, or a bear, or anything I want."

"Yeah, but what's your natural form? Even I know that shifters really have two forms—human and animal. What's your animal?"

"I'm a wild boar."

A snort escaped me that was, shall we say, less than ladylike. "When they say men are pigs, they usually don't mean it literally."

"I'm not a pig," he said, stiffening. "I'm a wild boar. It's a fearsome, dangerous animal."

"If you say so."

"I'm a very gifted shifter," he said. "I can take any form just as easily. Right now, I'm a lone wolf." His chest swelled with pride at those words. His pecs strained against his T-shirt, and in the cold starlight, I could make out the tiny points of his nipples through the thin fabric. I tried not to stare. I'd never noticed a guy's nipples before. But it was hard not to appreciate that hunk of muscle. He was a really, really well-built man. Even in my distress I couldn't help but notice.

"It doesn't matter," I said, tearing my eyes away from his chest. "I don't care what form you take. What matters is getting Granny back." With that, I turned away and stepped off the stone porch. I paused a moment, almost expecting something to burst out of the nearest bush and set upon me. But then I realized that all those sounds I'd heard might have been him. He'd followed behind to make sure I was okay, to make sure nothing grabbed me the way it had grabbed my grandmother.

Warmth spread in my chest knowing that he'd been watching over me, even when I didn't know it. It was the kind of thing Malik would do. But he'd been my best friend all my life, while this guy had no obligation to me, no reason to protect me. And yet, he had.

Just as I was giving him credit for all this kindness, he stepped in front of me, blocking my path, and crushed my goodwill with a skeptical look. "How are you going to get her back from an entire pack of wolves?" he asked.

"I have magic," I said, pride swelling my own chest.

"That's cute," he said. "But they captured her for a reason. They're not going to let her go just because you rush in there, wave your wand around, and sing your little song."

"It's a not a song, it's a chant," I said through clenched teeth.

"Yeah, okay, Little Red," he said with a smirk. "You're going to need more than a *chant*."

"Oh, yeah? Then tell me, since you know so well. What do I need?" I tossed my hair back, defiantly refusing to cover it with my cloak just because he teased me about it.

"I could tell you exactly what you need," he said, meeting my smirk with one of his own. "But what do I get out of it?" His eyes traveled down my body, and a quiver started deep within me. I didn't want to cover myself with my cloak, either—I wanted to throw it open, so he could see more of me, *admire* more of me.

"Let me guess," I said, standing my ground and staring up at him, refusing to be intimidated. "I need a big, strong man like you to protect me when I go rushing in there with my wand and my silly little chant?"

"Exactly," he said with a grin, undeterred by my defiance. He was missing a tooth behind his canine, and I'd have bet my own familiar that he'd lost it in a fight. He just looked like the kind of guy who enjoyed a good brawl.

"Okay, tough guy," I said. "What are we waiting for?" Pushing past him, I strode back toward wolf territory.

The man caught up with me seconds later. "I can't go rushing in there, either," he said. "I'm not one of their pack, remember? They'll kill a lone wolf for invading their territory."

"But you're so brave and strong," I said, batting my eyes at him.

"I'm also not a fool." His hand closed on my upper arm, his grip like iron.

I opened my mouth to speak, but for once, I held my tongue. My eyes met his, which were serious now. Something flickered in his gaze, but I didn't know him well enough to identify it. This was new to me. I knew everyone in the First Valley, had seldom met anyone from outside my own coven. I didn't know how to read strangers.

"Then who are you?" I asked at last.

"Efrain," he said. "And I may be willing to find you and warn you, but I'm not willing to die for someone I don't even know."

"Fine," I said. "But I'm willing to die for my grandma, so I'm going on."

"Wait," he said. "I can't let you walk into a death trap."

"Why not?" I asked. "You don't even know me, remember? Why do you care?"

"I don't know." He shrugged, turning to face the mountain ahead. "But I do."

His straightforward answer caught me off guard, took the edge off my certainty. "What do you suggest?" I asked. Maybe it wouldn't be so bad to have someone point out the way, tell me a bit about the wolves before I barged in. How many times had my mother told me to stop being reckless before someone got hurt? Maybe there was some truth to her warnings. If my mother was to be believed, if I merely stepped over the boundary into wolf territory, the big bad wolves would eat me all up.

"At least make a plan," Efrain said. "I can help you with that to ease my conscience before I send a naïve little girl into a werewolf lair, can't I?"

"Naïve?" I asked incredulously. "Little girl?"

"You look pretty little to me," he said with a shrug.

"I'm eighteen, thank you very much. I happen to be quite skilled as well. In fact, I'm probably stronger and more dangerous than you, even if I am a *little girl*."

"Oh, I don't know about that. I'm a very dangerous man," he said, stepping closer, until our bodies were just a breath apart. The animal warmth of his body leapt across the space between us, racing over my skin.

I shivered.

He chuckled quietly in the darkness. "Don't say I didn't warn you."

Chapter Four

Cayenne

We stood on the path arguing until I was shivering from the driving wind. In that time, Efrain had nearly convinced me that invading wolf territory in the middle of the night was not just suicidal, it might be dangerous for my grandmother if they figured out who I was.

"Let me draw you a map at the very least," Efrain said. I could hear his teeth chattering together when he spoke. We'd been standing there for fifteen minutes arguing about whether to go on tonight or wait until morning. And he was in a T-shirt.

"Fine," I said, turning back. "Let's go back to my grandma's cottage, and I'll build a fire."

"Thank all the gods," he said, rubbing his arms as we trekked back along the path. "It's colder than a witch's…well.

It's cold out here." He glanced sideways at me to see if I'd taken offense.

"Just to warm up," I warned. "You are not staying the night with me in my grandmother's house."

"Hey, you brought it up," he said, holding up both hands. "But now that you mention it…"

"Absolutely not."

"You going to make me sleep on the porch like a dog?"

"You are a dog, aren't you?" I shot back.

"I bet I could change your mind," he said, a haughty smile playing across his face.

"I'm sure you could," I said. "But it's not going to happen, so there's no point in trying."

"But you're sure I could?" he asked, still smirking. "What does that mean? That I look like the kind of guy who could make a girl say yes to anything?"

"You look like the kind of guy who's used to having girls say yes to anything," I said, stomping the dirt off my boots before stepping up the one step onto the stone porch. I turned the knob, and Efrain reached over my head to pull the door open for me. I rolled my eyes at the silly gesture— covens were well aware that women could open doors as well as men, and they didn't bother with such things. In fact, I could have summoned the wind and blown the door off its hinges if I wanted. But I felt a little dainty as I stepped through the door, which wasn't entirely unappreciated. No one had ever treated me like a delicate flower before.

"Let me get the fire started," Efrain said, approaching the stone fireplace. He laid the logs on, but as he bent to strike a match along the stones, I summoned the charge and snapped my fingers. Fire roared up around the logs. Efrain jumped back, stumbling on the rug Granny Golden had woven and lain on the floor before the hearth. He turned a scowl on me, and I smiled serenely back at him.

"Got anything to eat around here?" he asked, stalking over to the couch. Before I could protest, he picked up an apple and took a huge bite out of it.

"What'd you do that for?" I asked, rearranging the basket to fill the gap. "These are for my granny."

"I'm hungry," he grumbled, taking another quarter of the apple in one bite.

I shook my head. He was an animal, after all.

"Fine, eat the apples," I said, pushing the basket towards him. Still, I winced when he chomped into another one. But he had done a lot for me without asking more than some basic necessities.

"All right, let's hear this master plan of yours," I said as Efrain bit into his third apple.

"I said you needed a plan," he said through a mouthful. "I didn't say I had one."

I sat back on the sofa and crossed my arms. "Great. I'm feeding you all her apples for nothing."

"Apples are easy to come by," he said. "A wolf who's willing to help you? Not so much."

I paused a moment and then nodded. "You're right. I'm just worried about her. But we'll find a way to help her. She's…not well. I don't understand what they want with her. She doesn't even have magic anymore. She's just an herbologist."

Efrain cleared his throat and swallowed his mouthful. "There's an eclipse coming up."

"I know that," I snapped. Though witches didn't worship the moon the way werewolves did, we were in tune with the natural world. Many of us felt the magnetic pull of the full moon, like the ocean's tides, and noticed an increase in our abilities. The coven would honor the eclipse.

"I probably shouldn't be telling you this…" Efrain looked down at the gnawed apple in his hand, half of it gone in two bites. "Wolves don't like to share their traditions with outsiders."

"Is that why they shunned you? Because you tricked them into letting a shifter see their sacred ceremonies?"

"There's a reason for their secrecy," he said, glowering at his uneaten apple.

I sighed. "Just tell me why they took my grandma."

"They do a blood sacrifice at the eclipse," he said, growling the word through clenched teeth.

"What?" I said, my eyes widening in horror. I must have heard him wrong. Sure, the coven told stories to warn the children from crossing into wolf territory. But if they did human sacrifices, surely I would know.

But then…maybe not. Everyone knew that a full moon ceremony in which the people changed into wolves was the most sacred and private of rituals. No one who wasn't a werewolf was even allowed to witness it. Everyone had heard the story about Yvonne crashing one of their parties and being cast out in disgrace.

"It's usually someone old or sick, someone they can help along…" Efrain's eyes were glued to his hands. Suddenly, I wondered if he'd ever done the killing or if the pack leader was in charge of that.

"You mean someone helpless," I spat.

Efrain swallowed.

I found myself wanting to blast his face off with a fireball, so I curled my hands into fists. Sparks spit from between my fingers.

Efrain's eyes widened.

"How do you know?" I asked, my tone harsh against the soft roar and crackle of the fire. "Why should I trust you, if you're the kind of person who pushes an old lady into a fire, or eats her alive, or whatever the hell wolves do? If you're not a part of the pack, how do you know what they took her for?"

"I saw them take her," he said quietly, still not lifting his eyes to mine. "She was begging for her life, saying she had children, grandchildren… That's how I knew who you were. In my old pack, when there was an eclipse, we considered it enough to donate our blood." He held out the underside of his forearm to show me a long line of horizontal slash marks

29

scarred into his skin. He'd done a fine job of tattooing up the rest of his arms.

"I thought you said it was someone helpless."

"When we had a human sacrifice, it was a dying member of our own pack who chose to sacrifice himself to the goddess Diana that night, by his own hand. It was considered an honorable, sacred death if someone could die during an eclipse. But we didn't sacrifice outsiders. We didn't kidnap." At the last words, his tone bit through the warmth in the room and his lip curled in disgust.

"We have to get her back tonight," I said, jumping to my feet and snatching up the cloak I'd discarded as the room grew warmer.

Efrain held up a hand. "Tonight's not the eclipse. We should wait until morning, when we know they'll all be human, and we can sneak in without them smelling us. They have wolves patrolling their territory at night."

"But Granny—."

"Wouldn't want you to get yourself killed for her," Efrain said, his voice a quiet rumble.

He was right, of course. I paced the room while he finished off his fourth apple. I couldn't even think about eating. Everything in the room reminded me of Granny Golden, each memory hitting me like a punch to the gut. The woven rug in front of the fireplace with the two worn spots where Grandma knelt to start the fire each night. The needlepoint scenes hanging on the wall. One of them was sewn with messy, loose stitches, a white tiger that I had done when I was only eight. The sofa was covered in a throw my grandmother had crocheted. My father said that since she'd lost her magic, Granny's hands hadn't stopped moving. She had found ways to feel useful even without magic.

"We should get some sleep," I said as I stood before the fire, my eyes passing over the clay pots and vases my grandmother had made through the years, each sprouting bunches of dried herbs and flowers. Everything in its place even in her absence, though she couldn't remember to feed herself half the time.

"All right," Efrain said, heaving his giant frame from the sofa.

"You don't have to go," I said. "You take the bedroom, and I'll sleep out here and keep watch."

"Not a chance," he said. "I'll take the sofa."

I started to argue, but he'd already moved the basket off the cushion and draped himself over the sofa. His bulk dwarfed the small thing, and despite my distress, I couldn't help but smile at the way he seemed to be spilling off every edge of it. But I wasn't about to move that mountain of a man, and I needed a good night's rest if I was going to be fighting werewolves in the morning.

Chapter Five

Efrain

I stood over Cayenne's bed, watching her sleep. I wasn't proud of what I was doing, but that didn't mean I was going to stop. I'd done a lot of things I wasn't proud of. What were a few more marks against an already irredeemable man?

Her lips parted, and a soft breath escaped her. She looked so fucking sweet lying there in her grandma's bed, with the patchwork quilt pulled up to her chin. I had to remind myself she wasn't mine for the taking. I was delivering her, that was all.

If only I'd turned my back when she stepped into my path. Everyone knew better than to bargain with a witch. How many times had my own mother told me that? Never take a favor from a witch, never owe one, and for damn sure never offend one. You might steal some lettuce from a witch, and the next thing you knew, you owed her your firstborn child. If she crashed your party, you better give her a place of honor, because if you dared mention that she wasn't invited, she'd curse you and your children.

But damn if Cayenne wasn't one hot tamale. Her name just about fit her to a T, the spicy little thing.

Because it had been too damn long since I'd gotten laid, I hooked my finger under the edge of the blanket and peeked under. She was wearing a gauzy nightgown that left way too little to the imagination. It was probably something that belonged to her loony grandmother—a flowery, high-necked thing that would have stretched tight over a shapeless lump like her grandmother. But on her…

With a rush of shame, I tore my eyes away from the fabric skimming her curves and dropped the blanket.

"Hey," I said, shaking her awake. I made sure to keep my hands on top of the blankets. The last thing I needed was to fall under a witch's spell. "Hey, wake up. Someone's outside."

"What?" Cayenne asked groggily, staring up at me like she didn't know who I was.

"Someone came to the door," I said. "I think it was one of the wolves."

"Did they have Granny?" she asked, sitting up. The blanket fell around her waist, and I momentarily lost my train of thought. Her nipples looked like peaks of strawberry frosting.

"Uh—no," I managed. "They were looking for you."

"Me?" she asked. "How did they know I was here?"

"They must have been watching. When I wouldn't give you up, they ran off. But you can be damn sure they'll be back. We need to get out of here—now."

She shivered, the chill showing right through her nightgown.

"Bastards," she muttered, throwing off the blankets and exposing creamy white thighs. But I didn't have long to ogle her, because she jumped up and grabbed the dress she'd been wearing that day. "Let's see what they want."

"You can't just walk out there and give yourself up to them," I said. "It was stupid to stay here in the first place, in the same house where they took your grandma. We need to get the fuck out."

"No way," she said. "You can run away squealing, but I'm going to see what they want. They might negotiate for her release."

"You're crazy," I said. "You can't fight a pack of wolves."

"Watch me."

"You're going to get yourself killed," I said, regretting waking her at all. This wasn't going according to plan. Her grandma had made her sound malleable.

"I'm not afraid of werewolves," she said. "I have enough magic to burn their entire valley without breaking a sweat. And I'll do it if they won't give her back."

Now she was just delusional. Either that, or granny had lied to me when she told me the girl didn't have much magic.

Shaking out her drab, witchy garment, she stood up straight and scowled at me. "Do you mind?"

"Not a bit," I said, flashing her a grin.

"Out," she ordered.

I shrugged and retreated. A minute later, Cayenne appeared in the doorway. Her dress concealed every inch of her skin from the neck down, but now that I'd seen a little more of her, I saw how it hugged her shape in a way I hadn't noticed before.

"I know somewhere safe we can go," I said as a howl sounded outside.

Cayenne's eyes darted from the window back to me. "That sounded close."

"My brother's house is just over the ridge. Let's go."

A howl sounded again, so close it seemed to press into the cottage, filling the space around us.

Cayenne shivered. "What do they want?"

"They won't negotiate with you when they're in wolf form," I pointed out. "And if we don't get out of here, they'll break in through the windows or burn down the house. We've got to get out of here. *Now.*"

I ripped off my shirt, not missing the way Cayenne's eyes widened, her gaze locked o my ripped chest. Another howl sounded, this one so close my ears cringed in protest. A scrabbling sound came from outside the front door.

"Okay," Cayenne said. "But if they attack us, you'll see why I'm not scared of them."

"Be brave, not stupid," I said. "Sometimes the bravest thing to do is run."

She rolled her eyes, but I didn't wait for more. I grabbed her and slung her over my shoulder, ignoring her cry of surprise as I dove through the window in a shower of glass just as the front door exploded inwards.

Thinking quickly, I shifted into a stallion in midair, my remaining clothes exploding into tatters as I landed. Cayenne cried out in shock, clutching onto me for all she was worth. Snarls sounded inside the house, but I hardly heard them. I took off towards the Third Valley. I knew my brother wouldn't let me down, but I had to do my part to get her there.

My mind kept replaying my shift. I hadn't lied about that—I was the quickest shifter in the Third Valley. I heard Cayenne's gasp again as I swelled under her, pushing her higher off the ground and spreading her thighs with my body. Maybe a stallion had been a bad idea.

Her arms slid around my neck and she lay forward, holding on tight as I began to gallop. Her legs gripped my sides, and her shifting weight nearly drove me crazy. I could feel every muscle in her body moving with mine, the motion of her hips keeping rhythm with my stride, her legs wrapped around my girth.

I raced through the trees, along the path, trying to see where I was going. At last, I slowed. Cayenne sat up, laughing, and petted my neck. Burying her hands into my mane, she looked around, her hips moving in a slower rhythm on top of me. Fuck, this had been a bad choice. By the time I reached my brother's, I was in no state to shift to human.

I stopped outside the trailer outlined in the moonlight. Cayenne slipped from me, her breath coming in clouds in the night air. As I nuzzled her neck and, okay, a little lower, she laughed and wrapped her arms around me, scratching my ears. I took the opportunity to shift into human—I couldn't help myself. I wanted to feel her body against mine in the worst way.

I thought she'd jump back, but she stood there with her arms around me for a long moment, our bodies pressed together with just that dowdy dress between us. Inhaling deeply, I took in the scent of her hair, a mix of apples and spice and the freshness of the night around us. I wished she was wearing that thin nightgown again. Or maybe I didn't. There was no way I could control myself with her in that slip of cloth. She'd be flat on her back with her legs in the air in two seconds flat.

"What did they do to my grandma's house?" she whispered at last, breaking the spell that had fallen over us.

Before pulling away, I pictured her grandma to get myself under control. "I don't know," I said. "Let's get inside in case they follow us here."

"This is your brother's house?" she asked, looking at the trailer skeptically. "And this is supposed to keep us safer than my grandmother's house?"

"There's not a pack of wolves outside it."

"I don't think my mother would like that very much," she said. "I mean, it was one thing to let you stay at Granny's with me. But waltzing into a stranger's sketchy house? How do I know your brothers aren't going to ambush me?"

That didn't make a lick of sense to me, since I thought she didn't have a mother. Maybe she wasn't as competent as she seemed. Her grandma had given me the impression she might be mentally deficient. But Cayenne seemed sharp enough, if a little reckless.

"They're not going to gobble you all up, if that's what you're worried about."

"What are they?" she asked. "They're shifters, right?"

"Yeah. Wild boars like me."

She nodded, like this made sense. "Okay," she said. "I think I can hold my own against three pigs. Let's go meet them."

Chapter Six

Cayenne

My parents would freak if they saw me walking into a trailer with a strange man covered in tattoos. Now that he'd shifted and was leading me inside, I could see exactly how many tattoos. His arms, chest, and back were covered in ink. A giant bear snarled at me from the slab of muscle that formed one side of his back. The other side held a tower of fierce animal faces, like some kind of fearsome totem pole.

Below that, he had a tiny purple flower on one butt cheek, which was kinda cute. For some reason, it made me like him a little more. Under all those clothes, he had a flower tattooed on his ass. He must have a soft spot inside there somewhere.

At any other time, I might have welcomed the new sensations stirring inside me. They weren't exactly unpleasant. There was something irresistible about talking to a new person from a completely different world. I loved my fellow witches, of course, but the familiarity made conversation both easy and mindless. A stranger, on the other hand, held endless possibilities for discovery and danger.

The trailer was stuffy and small. I seriously doubted it would hold up to a pack of wolves for even one minute. They'd probably crush it like the tin can it was. There was a reason that tornados always blew away trailers. I was pretty sure Efrain could rock it hard enough to roll it over with just his weight.

A light went on when we walked in, and a guy appeared in the hallway. When he switched on the light in the tiny living room we'd entered, I couldn't help but smile. Where Efrain was all muscles and swagger, this guy radiated a relaxed confidence. He was also adorable, more angular than muscular, tall and lean, with a mop of messy bronze hair that almost concealed a pair of enormous ears. He was wearing a robe and a pair of well-worn slippers with pink pig faces on his giant feet.

I couldn't help but smile when my gaze met his twinkling blue eyes. When he returned my smile, a dimple sank into his left cheek. "Hey, there, little lady," he said, looking me over as I did the same to him.

"Hi," I said. "I'm Cayenne."

"Spicy," he said, still grinning.

"Yeah, sure."

"Not funny?" he asked, thrusting out a hand. "I'm sure you get that all the time. Must be annoying. I'm Oral. As you can imagine, I should know better than to make jokes about someone's name."

I had rarely been outside the First Valley, and when I did, it was to go shopping or do something fun with my family. I couldn't remember ever telling anyone outside the valley my name, and since everyone there knew me, I wasn't used to comments about my name.

"Cayenne wants to go into the Second Valley and get her grandma back from the wolves," Efrain said, emerging from a room behind me where he'd ducked to get dressed. "They kinda ran us out of her house, so we thought we'd come here and take refuge."

"Sure," Oral said, scratching his mop of hair. "Sorry I don't have the place cleaned up better. I wasn't expecting company."

"Doesn't look like you're too surprised to see your brother, either," I said, quirking an eyebrow at Efrain. "I thought you said you'd run off and joined some other pack."

"I did," Efrain said. "I told you I got exiled."

"Not much of a lone wolf," I said with a smirk. "Looks like you just ran home again."

"Damn," Oral said, clapping Efrain's shoulder. "She's as brutal as Violet."

"Who's Violet?" I asked.

"He didn't tell you about Violet? Bro, I thought you were going to see the wolves with her, not falling in love."

"I have a cousin named Violet," I volunteered.

"I'm not in love," Efrain growled, glaring at me.

"Then why didn't you tell her about Violet?"

Efrain turned his glare on his brother. "It didn't come up. Where's Nelson?"

"He heard some weird noises," Oral said, stepping around a small round table and into the kitchen. He opened an ancient brown refrigerator. "Would the lady like a beverage? I got cheap beer, Kool-Aid, and clamato juice."

"Oh, wow," I said. "I think I'll pass."

Oral laughed. "Kidding. I have soda, too. Grape and orange."

"I'm really more worried about finding my grandma and figuring out why they took her and why they're after me."

"She doesn't mess around," Oral said to Efrain. "I like her. If you marry her, can I be your best man?"

"I'm not marrying her," Efrain said, glowering.

"Are you sure? I gotta claim the best man spot before Nelson gets it."

"You're the worst man I know," Efrain said.

"Too bad you're stuck with me," Oral said, handing Efrain a beer. "But I don't buy the love bit. I'm pretty sure the last dozen times you've met a girl, you introduced yourself by whipping out a picture and asking if she'd seen Violet."

"Again, who's Violet?" I asked. If they weren't going to take me to find Granny Golden tonight, at least they could tell me a good story. Plus, I didn't really like the thought of Efrain mooning over some girl. I'd liked him better when he was mooning over me. It was stupid, I knew. He was a shifter, and I was a witch. But that didn't stop me from being attracted to him, despite his ability to rub me wrong at every turn.

"Violet is his ex," Oral said. "She ran off and left him, but he's sure his wit and charm will win her back if she'll just give him another chance."

"Shut up," Efrain said to his brother before turning to me. "That's not what happened."

"So, who is she?" I asked. "If that's not who she is."

He paused, then gave a disgruntled nod. "He's right," he said. "I didn't want to come out and ask you for a favor without helping you first. But I was going to ask if you'd help me find her. I heard the witches have an Eye of Odin."

"I don't think so," I said, shaking my head slowly.

"No, the witches call them seeing stones," Oral said.

"We don't have one," I said. A seeing stone was a faerie charm that someone could put behind a looking glass and see anyone in the world. I'd heard about them from my fae father, but he'd said we didn't have one.

"Oh," Efrain said, his shoulders slumping.

His dejection irked me, and I crossed my arms over my chest and glared at him. "So you weren't helping me because you were nice. You were helping me so I'd owe you."

"She got you, man," Oral said, clapping Efrain on the back again.

"It wasn't like that," Efrain said to me, but he ducked his head and wouldn't meet my eyes.

"Fine," I said. "It doesn't matter. Thank you for your help so far, but I can't get you a seeing stone, so you don't have to help me anymore."

I turned, swishing my cloak dramatically as I exited the trailer. I promptly stepped onto the wobbly cinderblock steps and pitched forward.

"Cayenne," Efrain called, lunging for me.

But he was too late. I leapt off the steps, fell, rolled, and ended up back on my feet.

"She's nimble, too," Oral said, grinning at me.

"Who's this?" asked a voice behind me.

I spun around to find a naked man standing behind me. No one was freaking out, so I had to assume he wasn't a wolf. "I'm Cayenne, who are you?"

"Their brother," he said, nodding at the others. "Nelson."

"Oh," I breathed, momentarily distracted by his naked body. He had a blond, military haircut and a strong jaw, piercing green eyes, and a generous…package.

He shot me a knowing look when he caught me staring.

"You don't look like the kind of woman who usually ends up here. Are you lost?"

"I'm…uh…visiting."

"You weren't that speechless when I shifted in front of you," Efrain grumbled behind me.

"Maybe because you're an ass," I shot back.

"I see you're well acquainted with my brothers," Nelson said. "Let me grab some clothes and we'll get acquainted, too."

"No hurry."

"Attire's optional around here," he said, looking me over with keen interest. "So if you'd rather get acquainted without them…"

"That might be distracting," I said, though I wouldn't have minded seeing him or his brother without clothes a little longer. In truth, Efrain was even more impressive, but I wasn't about to tell him that.

Nelson slipped past me, close enough that I could feel the heat of his body in the cold night, but not so close that I could touch him. I kinda wanted to. Okay, I really wanted to.

I closed my eyes for a second when he passed, catching a whiff of something wild and animal on the air. A shiver trembled through me, and I felt my nipples grow taut against the fabric of my dress.

I knew my mind was just trying to distract me from the horror of my grandma being taken. But that didn't make it any easier to resist the urge to reach out and trail my fingers across Nelson's sculpted abs. He had tattoos, too, though I couldn't make them out clearly in the dark. He only had a few instead of a whole coat of armor made of ink.

"Guess he didn't find anything out there," Efrain said.

"Are all shifters that brave?" I asked. "My parents would be casting a protection spell and forbidding me from going outside until noon the next day if they heard a weird noise."

"My brothers are brave," Oral said. "I'm more into, you know, staying alive."

"He's our little housewife," Efrain said, throwing an arm around Oral's neck. "He likes to make dinner and all that shit."

Oral grinned. "I'm telling you, it's why I get all the girls."

"I don't want a girl," Efrain said.

"So," I said, looking up at the two of them standing in the doorway. "I can't help you, which means you don't need to help me."

"We're still not going to let you go into wolf territory on your own," Efrain said before I could say it.

"Fine," I said, crossing my arms. "If you're not going to let me go get my grandma tonight, then you're going to have to entertain me. There's no way I can go back to sleep."

"I can think of a few ways to spend a night that do not involve sleeping," Oral said with a suggestive wiggle of his eyebrows. He and Efrain hopped out the door and into the yard, both of them leering down at me.

"We just met," I reminded them.

Oral grinned. "And?"

I tried to think of a response to that. Witches weren't promiscuous, at least not in our valley. Sex was sacred to us. I hadn't even slept with Malik, and we'd been best friends our whole lives. Only one of my friends had lost her virginity before adding a member to her collective, and she'd married him soon after.

"Let's try something a little less…intimate," I said.

Oral and Efrain started laughing like it was the funniest thing they'd ever heard in their lives.

"What's funny?" Nelson asked, stepping out the front door. He was wearing jeans and a Razorback hoodie now, and I had to admit, he looked pretty good in that, too.

"Nothing," I said, giving the others a pointed look.

"Cayenne needs something fun to do all night," Efrain said, giving me a truly wolfish look.

"Like planning how we're going to get my grandma back," I said through gritted teeth.

"Right," Oral said, his face twitching with suppressed laughter. "That was my first thought, too."

"You're all pigs," I said. "Literally and figuratively."

"Aw, don't be so hard on us," Oral said. "At least you know right up front what you're getting."

"Come on, have a beer and relax," Efrain said, taking my elbow and urging me towards a circle of canvas chairs arranged around a large firepit in the yard.

"Oral, grab us a couple, would you?" Nelson asked, tossing some logs into the ring of stones.

Warmth tingled up my arm from Efrain's fingers, and I tried not to think about what that meant, about how different it was from the feeling I had when Malik touched me. Malik made me feel comfortable and loved, but never like this— like he might grab me and devour me at any moment.

I shook that thought away. Efrain had a girlfriend somewhere out there. I didn't even know where the thought

TWISTED

had come from. It had just popped into my head. It wasn't like I was contemplating what it would be like if he did devour me.

Too soon, he released my arm, and I shivered, hugging myself. His touch had warmed me in ways I couldn't explain.

Oral returned to the trailer, and I could hear it creak as he trod across the floor. He appeared again a moment later as we all took seats around the fire. Wood and sticks were already piled into the circle of stones, so I summoned a little flame from the center to start it burning.

"Whoa," Nelson said. "Who did that?"

"This one's got all kinds of tricks up her sleeve," Efrain said, reaching out to pull my hood off.

"Hey," I protested, pulling it up, hiding the dopey grin on my face.

Oral handed around cans of beer. "Have a brew. Isn't that what witches drink?"

"I don't really drink."

"Just because you've never done something doesn't mean you can't," Efrain said with a smirk.

"Are you trying to corrupt me?" I asked, pulling my cloak around me.

"Just trying to loosen you up," he said. "Tight is hot, uptight isn't."

I felt my face burning at his overtly sexual comment, and I ducked my head, taking a deep breath to collect myself. This wasn't like me. I'd never blushed before in my life. I wasn't bashful. I had never been shy, and I wasn't going to let a herd of wild pigs change that.

Mom was the cautious one. I had yet to meet anything I couldn't defeat with my control of the elements. I was pretty sure a beer wasn't going to be my undoing. They were all sitting around slurping from their beers, and I wasn't going to wimp out and give them more reason to tease me. It was just glorified water, and I had full control of all things water. I could probably handle it better than they could.

I popped the tab and took a long swig. I gulped down the mouthful, just barely managing not to cough it all over the fire.

"Good, huh?" Oral asked, holding up his can to salute me from across the fire.

"It tastes like the water used to wash out a garbage can," I said, wiping my tongue on the back of my hand.

The guys all laughed. After a second's pause, I joined in. I started to relax, my mind dropping away from my grandma as the fire crackled and sparked into the night above us. The guys weren't exactly like the warlocks I knew, but maybe that was a good thing. I had barely left the witch community a dozen times in my life. These guys lived just over a mountain from me, and I'd never even met them.

Besides, what was the worst that could happen? It wasn't like they could hurt me. If they tried, I'd just throw a shield up and block them. And I seriously doubted that would be necessary. What were they going to do, flirt me to death?

Chapter Seven

Cayenne

"Tell us about your grandma," Nelson said a while later, watching me from across the fire.

"She's a non-magical witch," I said. "She had her magic stripped before I was born. It kinda made her a little…spacy. But she's the sweetest lady you'll ever meet.

"I didn't ask who she was," he said. "I said tell me about her."

I took a deep breath, hugging myself and letting the warm memories of her fill me until I thought I'd cry. I blinked back my emotions before speaking. "When I was a kid, my parents would bring me and my sisters over there and drop us off for a few days to help out. She'd put us up on stools at the counter with her and teach us how to make bread or pie crust or jam… Whatever she was making. She'd let us stay up as late as we wanted, and wherever we fell asleep, she'd find us and lay a blanket over us instead of disturbing us and making us go to bed. When I find the wolves who took her, they're going to learn just what a bad idea it is to cross a witch."

I could feel my eyes burning as my resolve hardened—the rare kind of heat that meant my eyes were glowing with stored up magic ready to be unleashed on someone.

"Damn," Efrain said, crushing his beer can in his bare hand. "Has anyone ever told you that you're kind of scary?"

"You have no idea," I said with a grin.

All my life I'd been warned about how strangers were dangerous and potentially evil, but it turned out, they were super friendly…and easily impressed.

"Who needs another beer?" Efrain asked, heaving himself out of his chair, his biceps bulging deliciously. I studied his bare arms, the firelight glimmering golden on his tan skin, dancing off a sleek cougar slinking down his forearm onto his hand.

"Sure, why not?" I said, tearing my eyes from his muscles. "You only run away from home once, right?"

"You ran away from home?" Oral asked.

"Not technically," I said. "But I probably should have gone back when I found out my grandma was gone."

"Why didn't you?" Nelson asked. There was no judgment in his voice, only curiosity as he waited for my answer.

"I…I don't know, really," I said, squirming under his scrutiny. "It was night, I guess, and I didn't want to walk home in the dark. It would take a couple hours to get back. And then you showed up and offered to help." I looked up at Efrain, who was hovering, listening to me instead of going to get the beers.

"And?" he asked, his eyes riveted on mine.

"And maybe I'm a little tired of being the good little witch who does what she's told, helps her granny, and doesn't talk to strangers." I dropped my gaze to the fire and hunched my shoulders, guilty for saying such a thing even though I fully realized the truth of my words as I said them.

"We've been known to turn a few good girls bad," Oral said, grinning when our eyes met.

"I don't think going to save my granny counts as being a bad girl."

Efrain bent and whispered in my ear, "It's what you do on the way."

A wonderful tingling spread through my body, and I closed my eyes and savored it.

With a chuckle, he straightened and jogged to the trailer, disappearing inside.

"I just don't want my parents to worry," I said, hearing how much that sounded like an excuse even as I said it to the others. "If I tell them about Granny, they'll freak out. They get so worked up about everything, especially people being kidnapped. I have enough magic to get her back without anyone else getting involved."

"Or maybe you wanted to run away and drink beer around a bonfire at three in the morning with three hot dudes," Oral said, wiggling his eyebrows at me.

I laughed, my brain feeling loopy and my body buzzing from the beer. "Maybe a little," I said. "It's just…I've gone on trips. It's not like I've never been out of Arkansas. But I've never had an adventure, you know? One that didn't involve a caravan of parents and siblings. Maybe I wanted a different kind of adventure."

"You came to the right place for that," Nelson said.

Just then, a howl ripped the fabric of the night, echoing through the forest around us and across the valley. It was so close that it yanked every hair on my body straight up, and I jumped to my feet.

"Shit," Nelson said, already on his feet. "I knew I heard something earlier." He ripped off his shirt, his muscles tensed to spring, and for the second time that night, I found myself staring at a man's nipples. The firelight glanced off the ridges of his muscles as he unbuttoned his jeans.

I gulped in anticipation.

"Let's get inside," Oral said, scooting around the fire and scooping me into his arms like he was going to carry me across the threshold of his trailer.

"Um, excuse me?" I said. "I can put a shield around us that will protect us a lot better than your trailer. And I can certainly walk."

"Are you sure?" he asked. "You sound a little tipsy."

Another howl tore into the night around us, lonesome and tortured as it came even closer. The firelight glimmered off a pair of eyes in the trees, and I gripped Oral's neck involuntarily.

"Besides, it's not every day that I get to sweep a beautiful woman off her feet."

"Your trailer looks like the next gust of wind could sweep it off its feet," I said. "Or wheels."

Instead of laughing, his nostrils flared as he scented the air. "Quick, get on Nelson's back and he'll get you out of here," he said. "We'll distract them."

Before I could ask, a gigantic, hideous boar appeared beside us. I screamed.

"It's Nelson," Oral said urgently, depositing me on its bristly back. It stood as high as my waist, its tusks like the curved blades of ivory swords. He started forward, and I lurched, throwing myself flat on his back and wrapping my arms around his neck. I clung to him as I'd clung to Efrain on the ride here, and he took off, streaking onto the road and charging along at breakneck speed.

Unlike when I'd ridden Efrain, it wasn't exhilarating and a little bit exciting, knowing I was literally riding a man. Nelson's spiny bristles poked through my dress, rubbing me raw as he ran. The beer sloshed in my belly, making me feel a little sick. The pavement blurred by beneath his feet, and barren trees whipped in the wind overhead. Cold wind tore my hood off, but I didn't dare to let go and pull it back on, even as my cheeks and ears ached with the icy air streaming across my face and through my hair.

At last, we turned onto a narrow gravel driveway. Trees overhung it on both sides, almost hiding it from the road. When we stepped out of the woods onto a grassy lawn, Nelson came to a stop. I gingerly lifted myself from his back, tugging my dress away from the raw skin of my thighs.

Looking up at the large rectangular stone house, I was comforted in a way I hadn't been at Oral's trailer. I could tell that this was a safe place. Strong, good energy surrounded it, though it didn't look particularly impressive. It was a simple two-story structure with windows along the top and bottom floors but no other features whatsoever, like it was modeled after a giant box. The red and tan stone looked solid enough that it might have stood in that spot for a few centuries.

I could blast it apart in seconds.

The boar swiftly turned to a man before my eyes, and even though I'd known it was Nelson, I still gasped in shock and took a step back. Sure, I used magic all the time, but I was used to my magic. Controlling the elements was one thing. Changing your entire body from one thing to another in three seconds flat was another.

"Wow," I said. "Color me impressed."

Nelson grinned. "I tend to have that effect on women."

"Do you also have the effect of making them bleed?" I asked.

"Depends on what we're doing."

A wolf's howl cut through the night, interrupting us.

"Shit," he said, his eyes going wide. "They must have followed our scent. Let's get inside."

Behind us, a snarl sounded, and I spun to find myself face to face with a charging wolf. I threw up my hands, and a stone shot out of the earth and slammed into the wolf's face just as Nelson's arm circled my waist and he swept me into the house. The door slammed, and I heard the wolf hit it with a thud. Nelson leaned back against the door, breathing hard, his arm still around me.

For a minute, we stood in silence. I could feel every inch of my body pressing against Nelson's, could feel his heart thundering against my back. The darkness inside was so complete I felt as if I weren't attached to my body at all. Whatever happened to it, I wouldn't be affected.

Robin fluttered a wing fitfully against my neck, and I realized with a start that my magic was suppressed here. I could feel the safety of the house, the magic in it, but it had overridden my own magic.

A wolf howled outside again, and Nelson's arm tightened around me, pulling me tighter to him. His free hand stroked my hair back, then grazed my shoulder and down my arm. A chill went through me and I melted against him without thought.

"That was a pretty cool trick you did out there," Nelson said quietly.

"It wasn't a trick," I said, my eyes opening. "It's elemental magic. Speaking of which, why can't I use it in here?"

Nelson hesitated. "I thought Efrain said you didn't have much magic."

I pulled away, indignant. "Excuse me? Just because I don't go around levitating and casting spells constantly doesn't mean I don't have magic. I'm the most powerful young witch in the valley, I'll have you know. I could light up your house like a beacon, and all the witches in the First Valley would come running."

Or could I? My pulse sped at the thought. Without my magic I was unarmed, defenseless.

Like Granny Golden.

"Let's not do that," Nelson said. A light flared, and the acrid smell of matches filled the air as he lit a candle. Warm light glimmered along the lines of his naked body, and I made out a snake tattoo winding around his bicep.

"You don't like witches?" I asked, swallowing hard. According to my parents, most people didn't. It was one of the reasons we never left our valley. Still, it was different to face that reality than to hear it spoken by paranoid parents.

"One of them is growing on me," he said with a glance my way.

"Whose house is this?" I asked. "And again, what's with the magic block?"

"Mine," Nelson said, ushering me to follow him down a hall. "When our dad died, he gave us each something. My brothers got money, but I wanted the house."

"Your brothers have money?" I asked, following close as another wolf howl ripped through the night. I looked down and realized how close to his muscular backside I was. "Not that I care. Witches don't really care about that kind of thing. It's just that if they had money, I wouldn't have expected them to live in a trailer."

"I said they *had* money," Nelson said. "Not that they still have it. They made some bad investments. Now, let's get you cleaned up."

"Like a lot of tattoos?" I asked.

He set the candle on the sink in a small bathroom and opened a cabinet, pulling out a wash rag. "Tattoos, booze, gambling, women, bribery, you name it," he said, running water over the cloth. "My granddad built this house with his own hands. And he had an enchantment put on it to protect it. Which means you're safe here, with or without your magic."

"Safe is a relative term," I said, watching his every move. I felt naked and vulnerable without my magic. But also, a strange freedom in putting my trust in him more completely than I'd ever had to do before.

"Sit over there and I'll fix you up."

"I can heal myself," I said, realizing his intent. I wasn't prudish—witches didn't have many hang-ups—but I'd just met Nelson. And now my life, my safety, my body, was completely in his hands and at his mercy.

"Yeah, but this is more fun," he said, turning from the sink. He picked me up around the middle and stepped to the tub while I protested, my toes skimming the floor. My heart thudded as Nelson sat me on the edge of the tub and knelt before me. "Okay, show me where I pricked you."

I hesitated, my breath coming faster in the too-small room. Candlelight flickered off Nelson's hair, spinning it to gold. I couldn't see his eyes clearly with the light behind him, but the hunger in them was clear and irresistible. He was waiting for me, wanting to tend to me. Wanting me for something that had nothing to do with my magic.

"If you won't show me, I can't be held responsible for my boar's bristles and what they did to you on the way here," he said. A smile quirked the corner of his mouth, but his eyes betrayed him. The longing I saw there was so deep, so fierce, it hurt to look at him.

Holding my breath, I curled my hands into the fabric of my skirt, drawing it slowly up my calves to my knees. Nelson swallowed so hard I could hear it in the little stone bathroom. I drew the skirt up higher, over my thighs, watching Nelson watching me. A new kind of power was stirring inside me, one I'd never known I had. Not witch magic, but something like it. My own power, as a woman.

Nelson slowly reached out, his cold hands closing around my knees. He eased them open, drawing a long, slow breath.

I looked down to see little red pinpricks dotting my fair skin like a rash from my knees to the apex of my thighs. Nelson licked his lips quickly, then picked up the wash cloth. Balling it between his fingers, he dabbed gently at the redness. The water was warm, soothing the raw skin. I swallowed hard, watching him work his way from inside my knee to the curve of my thigh.

As his fingers brushed my skin, shivers climbed my body, from the spot that he touched to my center, straight up through my belly and my chest, spreading out along my arms and up to the crown of my head. A trembling uncertainty built in my stomach, a nervousness that I'd never felt before.

This wasn't like me. I was sure and strong. I'd never doubted myself before, had never doubted Malik. But Malik had never set my body on fire with a thousand pinpricks. He had never touched me so slowly that I could hardly breathe with the anticipation of the next inch of my skin he'd cross.

Nelson had opened my skin, wounded me. Now he healed me with his touch, with the cauterizing heat of his desire. Each miniscule drop of blood was turned to flame by a kind of magic I didn't understand. Sparks rose through my body like they had from the bonfire, but these ones grew and multiplied inside me, cascading along the underside of my skin like a thousand falling stars. His fingers slowed, kneading my flesh, the washcloth dropping to the floor.

He hesitated, his eyes flicking up to mine. Every nerve in my body was alive, hungry. Ready. Nelson's fingers shook as they skimmed across the last inch of my thigh.

Chapter Eight

Cayenne

The front door burst open, followed by cursing and a flurry of movement that sent Nelson shooting to his feet. A growl of frustration built in my throat. We'd barely started, and now it was over.

"Nelson, are you in here?" Oral called. "I think Efrain's hurt. He was attacked."

"I'm here," Nelson said, stepping to the door. He turned back, his eyes tumultuous with emotion.

I threw my dress down over my knees, stumbling to my feet. The whole night was coming apart around me in ways that my magic couldn't fix.

"I have to go," Nelson said quietly. "You can sleep here if you want...? My bedroom is upstairs."

"I'm okay," I said, pushing past him. I led him down the hall, my mind tumbling with confusion. This wasn't over. I needed Efrain to be okay, so he could help me get Granny. Whatever had happened with Nelson was just a hiccup, something I could deal with later. I put it aside and focused on Efrain's figure, crumpled on the ground just outside the door.

"What happened?" I asked, approaching slowly, as if he might wake up and devour me.

"One of the wolves," Oral said with a grimace. He was naked, like the other two. Without clothes, his ropey muscles didn't bulge like Efrain's but wound around his long, lean frame. A smattering of freckles was strewn across his pale shoulders, and his smiling face was now grim.

Nelson's hand grazed my back. "You said you could heal yourself," he said. "Can you help?"

"Maybe," I said, stepping outside. Relief washed over me with the return of my magic. I crouched next to Efrain. "I'm not a water witch. They're the healers. I only know a little of their magic…"

"Can you try?" Oral asked, pleading in his eyes that made my heart hurt.

"Yeah, but…healing a little rash on my legs is one thing. Healing a wolf attack…"

"Help me roll him over," Oral said. "I don't know what happened. I found him like this."

I swallowed, feeling sick as Nelson and Oral gently rolled him over. I tried not to stare at his huge, muscular body, the tattoos climbing his arms, spreading across his broad chest and shoulders. I'd seen lots of naked people before—our coven didn't generally use bathing suits when we swam, since it was just us—but no one who looked quite like Efrain. He was so…big.

"I don't see any teeth marks," Nelson said, grabbing Efrain's chin and moving it from side to side. "But he definitely took a blow to the head."

"One of them must have thrown him," Oral said, his face going a little green as he eyed the giant lump on Efrain's forehead. The skin had split, and blood trickled down his forehead on both sides. Dirt was caked into the wound.

I fought to swallow, panic seizing inside my chest. "Was he…was he in pig form?" I asked, my voice coming out small and shaky like a child. "Or wolf?"

"He was chasing the wolves," Oral said. "Why?"

"In wolf form?"

He shrugged. "Yeah. Efrain can shift into anything else as easy as he shifts into a boar."

I touched Efrain's forehead, my fingertips shaking. I'd done this. I'd thought he was a bad wolf attacking us, so I'd bashed his head with a rock. He'd just been trying to run inside with us.

"Efrain, you idiot," I whispered, my throat tight. He'd been kind of an ass, but he'd protected me. He'd stayed with me at Granny's house, and then taken me to his brother's house to protect me. He'd stayed behind to ward off the wolves while I came here, and I'd hurled a rock at his head instead of letting him come in with us. And then, while he lay bleeding and unconscious in the yard, I'd shared an intimate moment with Nelson.

"Can you fix him?" Oral asked.

I didn't want to tell them that I'd done this to their brother. I nodded mutely, vowing to use all the magic I had to use to keep him alive. He was still breathing. His strong, thick chest rose and fell under the shroud of tattoos.

"I'll try," I said, scooting down beside him. I lay my head on his shoulder and snuggled close, closing my eyes. I let my palm slide across his warm skin, finding the heartbeat in the center of his chest.

"Damn," Oral said. "If that's how you heal someone, sign me up for the next attack."

"Shut up," Nelson said. "Let her concentrate."

My parents had always told me that healing energy was love energy. I pushed away my guilt and desperation, concentrating instead on the strong, healthy heartbeat inside him. For a minute, I let myself remember all the good things I knew about Efrain—his sense of humor, his kindness to a stranger, his protectiveness and loyalty to his girlfriend.

Unfortunately, that thought brought some less generous feelings, and I had to start over.

Once I had only good thoughts in my mind, I wrapped them around Efrain, sliding my arm over his broad chest and hugging him tight. I fed all the love I could into him, moving it into every part of his body that touched mine. All that energy I'd built up in the bathroom with Nelson softened, turning to healing warmth. The sparkles that had built inside my body now mellowed into soft strands wrapping around Efrain's body with unbearable tenderness.

With that energy still radiating from me, I lifted my hand and laid it gently across his forehead. I let the energy turn into magic, flowing like water from my fingertips. Releasing a rush of love and magic into him, I sighed and melted against him. No wonder my parents hadn't let me practice healing magic on anyone outside our family. It was powerful stuff.

My head was in a fog as Efrain's eyes fluttered open. Without so much as glancing around to see where we were, he rolled over onto me, his heavy body crushing down on mine. "What are you doing to me there, Little Red?" he asked, his voice slurry, his eyes unfocused.

"Saving your life," I said, forcing the words out in a normal tone. But there was nothing normal here. My heart was racing, my body charged with the energy buzzing between us.

A slow smile spread over his lips, and he brushed my hair back with both hands. "Can I show my thanks by eating you all up?"

His growled words sent a thrill shimmering through my body. It was all I could do not to arch up against him, wrap my legs around him. Instead, I stroked my fingers across his forehead, eliciting a groan from him. I cupped his rough, stubble-laden cheek with one hand, marveling at how small and dainty my hand looked against his rugged face. "We've got an audience," I whispered.

"They'd probably enjoy it as much as we did," he said, his fingers skimming my throat, sending a shudder of pleasure through me.

"That's just the residual magic talking," I said quickly.

His eyelids were heavy, his pupils dilated. "Did you put a spell on me? Whatever you did to me, I'm not sure I like it."

"No," I said, squirming under him. "I just healed your head."

"I don't appreciate people fucking with my head," he said, holding me captive as I squirmed. Every part of his body was giant and hard as steel. I wasn't scared, though. I could have used magic to break his hold. But I didn't. I was too excited by the strain of his hard body against mine, the heat of it, the need in it.

"I didn't," I said faintly. "I'm not."

"Now I know why they say witches are dangerous," he said, rolling off me. He lay on his back, not trying to hide the fact that he had enjoyed our contact as much as I had. And oh wow. If he felt big, he looked even bigger. I gulped, my heart liquifying in my chest at the thought of lying under him without my dress between us.

I averted my eyes, my cheeks warming. Oral grinned and held out a hand to me. "You can put a spell on me any time," he said, pulling me to my feet. "I enjoy people messing with my mind."

"I'm not," I protested again. He and Nelson had slipped away to put on clothes while I healed Efrain, and their state of dress both relieved and disappointed me, much to my chagrin. I wasn't sure about the fact that they'd left me alone with Efrain, either, or that they'd come back to watch.

"You know, shifters aren't strictly monogamous, either," Oral said with a wink. His hair had been mussed by the wind and the T-shirt he'd pulled on, and his big ears stuck out through his hair in the most adorable way. I wondered if he liked to have them nibbled, and then pushed away the ridiculous thought. I'd never wanted to nibble on a guy's *anything* before in my life. I wasn't usually so boy-crazy—at all. It was as if being around all these animals had unlocked my own animal side. I hadn't decided whether that was a good or a bad thing.

Right now, it was distracting the hell out of me, though.

"I think we need to concentrate on getting my grandma out of the Second Valley," I said. "Then we can talk about how much it would freak my parents out if I told them I wanted to add a shifter to my collective."

"That sounds like a fair deal," Oral said, with another of his easy smiles.

Efrain sat up, a fierce frown on his face. "I thought you didn't have parents," he said. "I thought you just had a grandma."

"Where'd you get that idea?"

"From the way your grandma was talking when I saw her," he said. "Maybe she was just trying to save her own skin."

"Well, I'm going to save it for her," I said. "And I'm practically like a daughter to her. So tell me what you know, and I'll go in tomorrow during the eclipse and get her out. Those wolves will never know what hit 'em."

"You can say that again," Nelson muttered.

Chapter Nine

Oral

Nelson set some candles on the table and we all sat around it. My dumb-ass brother was still bleeding, and he'd even gotten himself some spooning for it. The bastard. Now he was just about drooling over Cayenne. Not that I blamed the guy—she was a hot little firecracker, like her namesake.

"So, what's your plan?" Efrain asked, looking at her like she might share the wisdom of the universe. Whatever she'd done to him, it was hilarious. He'd be hearing about this one for years to come.

"I thought you were the man with the plan," I said. "Or did it all get knocked out of your head when that witch put her spell on you?"

"I didn't put a spell on him," Cayenne said with an exasperated sigh.

"It's called walking by with a pair of legs," Nelson said. "Don't take it personally."

"Shut up, asshole," Efrain said. "I'm doing this to find Violet. That's it."

"Sure you are," I said. "Then I guess you won't mind if I invite Cayenne to share my room tonight."

"Why would I?" he asked through clenched teeth, his hand fisting on the edge of the table.

I grinned. "Sweet. Cayenne, darling, would you like to share the guest room with me tonight? I'll be a total gentleman, unless you're curious about why I have such an unusual name."

Efrain's face darkened, and his shoulders just about ripped through the T-shirt Nelson had given him. Cayenne darted a glance back and forth between us, then fixed her eyes on Nelson.

"Can we get back to my grandma?" she asked.

There were a lot more interesting things on my mind, but I didn't want to offend the lady, so I kept my mouth shut for the moment.

I didn't know why Efrain was playing with this witch on the day we were going to invade the wolves' valley, but I couldn't ask until I got him alone again. He'd managed to avoid the question on the way over by shifting and running off before I could ask. Now I was dying to know, but in the meantime, I figured I could have some fun with this little witch.

"We can get up early and go into the valley while the wolves are sleeping," Efrain said. "Scope out the place, see if there's anywhere that they might be keeping your grandmother. Rumor has it they have a holding cell for wolves who misbehave."

"Have I mentioned how glad I am that we're shifters and our leader doesn't give an actual fuck about anyone but himself?" I said.

"They say their leader has a cage made of silver, the only thing that's strong enough to hold a werewolf when they shift," Efrain said.

"It's just a rumor," Nelson said, noticing that Cayenne had gone a little pale before I caught on. Damn. I had to get ahead in something. My brothers had me beat in the looks and size department.

"The wolves mostly keep to themselves," I said. "No one knows much about them."

"Except Efrain," Cayenne said, turning to my brother.

"I infiltrated a different pack," he said. "They have their own customs."

"Okay, so my grandma might be in a silver cage somewhere in the leader's house," Cayenne said. "We'll sneak down into their valley and see if we can find out where they're keeping her. Then we break her out, and—."

"In broad daylight?" I asked. "You don't think they'll have a single person standing guard, especially since this is their big day?"

"It'll be the middle of the day," Efrain said. "They'll be in human form, so they won't be as quick to sense our presence. And they'll be busy with their eclipse prep."

"And if they do notice you?" Nelson asked.

"Then we'll fight or run," Efrain said.

"You're going to take a little girl right into the middle of a pack of wolves?"

Cayenne scoffed. "Trust me, I can take care of myself."

"Oh, it's not you I'm worried about," I said. "Let's just say my brother is notorious for making stupid, rash decisions. Not sure you want to go along with him. Maybe he can scope it out, and you could stay here with me. You'll be safe, and I'll get to enjoy your company."

"She wants her grandmother back," Nelson said. "Quit flirting."

"Exactly," Cayenne said, but she shot me a smile.

"And what if you can't find your grandma?" I asked. "Or you can't spring her from the silver cage?"

"Then we'll lay in wait for them to take her out of the cage," Efrain said, his jaw set. "And then we'll make our move."

"Before the eclipse?" Nelson asked, eyeing our brother. Obviously he wanted to know what Efrain had up his sleeve, too. Was he planning to skip out when the invasion started? Get himself captured so we had an excuse to attack? And where did the girl tie in? She'd told him she couldn't help him find Violet, and he was still trying to get her grandma back.

We'd gone along with driving the girl here when he'd said it was for the invasion, but it was time for him to spill the beans about the rest of the plan.

"Whenever we find my grandma, we'll stay with her," Cayenne said. "We'll get her out as soon as we can."

"I'll be a lookout," I said, and all eyes turned my way.

"You don't have to do that," Cayenne said.

"None of us do," I said with a shrug. "Maybe you got me under your spell, too."

"We'll all go," Nelson said. "Not like we have anything better to do tomorrow." He gave Efrain a pointed look, but Efrain ignored him.

"You two stay here until the eclipse," Efrain said. "The more of us who go in, the more likely they'll hear us."

They laid out the plan a little further, but I was yawning by now. It was close to dawn. "Let's all get a few hours of sleep before we start," Nelson said. "We have a big day tomorrow."

"There's only two bedrooms in working order," I said, turning to Cayenne. "Wanna share mine?"

"The lady gets her own room," Nelson said, though he looked like he might be as bewitched as the rest of us.

"I don't want to put anyone out," Cayenne said. "You're already helping me way more than necessary. I'll just sleep on the couch."

"Me, too," I said with a grin.

"Won't bother me," she said. "I'm so tired I won't even notice you're there."

Nelson and Efrain laughed, but I just shook my head. "Oh, you'll notice."

"Seriously, Cayenne, it's not a problem," Nelson said. "Take one of the beds."

"I've slept on the couch before," Efrain said, sharing a look with her.

"If you insist on being uncomfortable, I can't stop you," she said. "I'm not going to fight you for the couch."

Twenty minutes later, Nelson was in his room and Efrain was snoring on the couch. Cayenne was in the guest bedroom, invitingly alone.

I tapped on the door and stuck my head in, then froze with my mouth half open. She had peeled off her dowdy dress and was standing beside the bed in her underwear. "Do you mind?" she asked, snatching the blanket up to cover herself.

"Can I come in?" I slipped into the room and pushed the door closed behind me.

For a second, our eyes met, and we stood caught in indecision. Finally, she sighed. "I meant what I said. I need sleep."

"I know," I said. "I'll even help you sleep better. Send you into sweet dreams all relaxed and happy."

"So you're offering a free massage?"

"I can massage you anywhere you want, baby."

"Shoulders would be good," she said, dropping onto the bed with an evil grin.

"Shoulders it is," I said, joining her on the bed. I scooted in behind her and pulled her into my lap. She resisted only a moment, then lay back against my chest. Her chili pepper-colored curls fell down her back, tickling my arms as my fingers worked the knots in her shoulders. Her body felt heavy against my groin, reminding me of how little separated us. I must have been crazy when I'd had this idea.

"Why do I get the feeling your hands are going to start wandering?" she asked after an agonizing minute of silence.

I placed a hand on my heart. "You don't trust that I can be a gentleman? I'm hurt."

"Says the man who conned his way into my bed awfully fast."

"Where I am selflessly serving you without a mention of anything in return."

"I can return the favor," she said. "Witches are a very fair people."

Remembering the tales I'd heard about witches exacting revenge, I shook my head. "That's really not necessary," I said. "It's my pleasure to serve."

"What if I insist?" she asked, twisting around to smile over her shoulder at me.

"Please don't. There's only so much a man can take."

She laughed and turned forward again, lying her head back against my shoulder. With a sigh, she closed her eyes. Minutes later, she was asleep.

I had some shameful thoughts lying there under her, I won't deny. There was a reason most of the women in our valley called us pigs, and it wasn't because of our animal form. The shifter community wasn't as tight-knit as the wolf one, but it was small enough that we all knew each other. Most women stayed away from us, having learned either by experience or hearsay that they didn't want to get mixed up with the likes of us. Those who did knew exactly what they were getting, and we gave them what they came for.

This little witch had no idea who she was dealing with. She didn't deserve the kind of rough treatment we usually dealt. She was from a community that was all about peace and love and respect. She probably didn't even know that we were any different, that shifters didn't partake of such notions. It didn't seem right to dispel that notion, but it left me in an uncomfortable situation.

At first, my body buzzed with the instinct to take what I wanted from her. I could make her want it, in the moment at least. She might hate herself in the morning, but that wasn't my problem. She might hate me, too, but that also wasn't my problem. Our valleys were next to each other, but I'd gone twenty years without seeing her, and I could go twenty more if I wanted.

But if I woke her, I'd erase whatever idea of me she had formed in her mind, however untrue. Whatever she thought of me, something told her it was okay to let me climb in bed with her in the first place, made her feel safe enough to fall asleep in my arms. She was so adorably naïve. Maybe I'd be doing her a favor to erase that. But I didn't want to—not yet.

For now, I might enjoy having someone look at me as more than the ugly little brother who picked up the sloppy seconds of his older siblings and left them sloppier than he'd found them. I was the guy who made pancakes and let them cry on his shoulder in the morning. I was the guy who gave them just enough sympathy that, in their vulnerable state, they'd give in one more time. Then I'd send them on their way, just as my brother had done. They'd leave with their heads hung in shame, having been duped not once but twice by the shameless boar brothers.

Cayenne didn't know all that. To her, I was just a shifter. To her, I had nothing in my past but a blank slate. I didn't want that to end just yet. Which left me stuck under her, too keyed up to sleep but unable to find release. After a while, I calmed down and just lay there, with my arms around her. Holding an innocent woman filled me with an odd sensation, a strange mixture of vulnerability and hunger. I'd never questioned what to do with a woman in bed before. I'd sure as hell never held one without itching to get her out of there at the earliest opportunity.

Now I had time to think, time to question why that was. I didn't come up with anything pretty. But Cayenne's trust in me gave me hope. What would it be like to be an honorable man, one worthy of that trust? Could I still be that man, despite what I'd done in the past? Or was it too late for redemption?

Chapter Ten

Efrain

Like so many stories, this one started with a girl. That's how I'd gotten into this unholy mess in the first place.

Sun sparkled in the rust on the dull splitting maul, and I paused, a pain tightening my chest at the thought of her. Even three years later, I could remember every day we'd spent at the river. The exact shade of her violet eyes, the way they'd flash dark when I splashed her as she lay sunning herself on the bank while I swam. The way her hair shone like a kaleidoscope of color as we lay on the riverbank together, each strand a different shade—amber and rust and auburn and gold. The mischievous smile that lit up not just her eyes but her whole face just before she shifted into a cat at the snap of her fingers.

Of course, then she'd squirm from my embrace and dart away, leaving my arms empty and streaked with blood from her razor-sharp claws.

I shook that thought away, guilt flaring in my gut like indigestion at the less-than-generous memory. I wouldn't dwell on the bad. Only the good. My childhood friend, neighbor, sweetheart. When she disappeared, no one knew what had happened to her, where she'd gone, or how to find her.

But now… Now I had a lead. All I had to do was get this job done, and I'd get what I'd been waiting for these three long years. I would have the answer. I would know who had taken her, and where they'd gone. Then I'd go after them.

I wouldn't imagine what she'd been through since her abduction, how she might have changed, what scars she now carried. Each time those thoughts rose in my mind, I blocked them with all the fierceness of a wolf defending his mate.

She was fine, and I would find her, and I would rescue her. End of story.

And yet, each step I took towards finding her left me further from the truth. It had started out simple enough.

Find out where she went.

Rescue her.

When the shifter king had returned to the valley just months after her disappearance, I'd been sure I'd get answers. They said he had a seeing stone, that he could find anyone in the world. Everyone had so much hope then. The prodigal king had returned. All would be well again. But when I'd asked for answers, the bastard had blown me off. It wasn't until I forced his hand that he'd agree to help. Even then, he had his own price. If he was going to help me find the missing shifter girl, I had to help him.

Desperate, I'd agreed to anything his greedy heart desired. King Owen had taken his time, toying with me until I thought I'd go mad. Finally, he had given me a task. Go into the valley of the wolves and bring back his daughter. I'd known a suicide mission when I heard it—a shifter against a pack of wolves.

But after searching for Violet on my own turned up not the slightest glimpse of a lead, I'd come home and gone back to see him. I'd agreed to his suicide mission. Life without hope was too cruel to endure, and not knowing what had happened to her, if she was alive or dead, was unbearable.

And so, the task had taken on another step.

Bring the king his daughter.

Find out where Violet had gone.

Rescue her.

I leaned the sledge against the side of the woodshed and wiped a forearm across my brow. The thought of adding the hapless, naïve witch inside the house to my plan made my stomach turn again. I should leave. Turn tail and run, leaving the redheaded witch better than I found her, with a clue to follow and my brothers both clearly smitten with her. That was the right thing to do. That's what a good man would do.

But I wasn't a good man. And all I wanted was Violet, the right thing be damned.

Getting the kimg's daughter had almost been a suicide mission. It would have been if the witch grandmother hadn't been there to save me. And now I had one more debt to pay off, one more step in my plan.

Bring the witch her daughter.

Bring the king his daughter.

Find where Violet went.

Rescue her.

I bent and began to pile wood into my arms. When I straightened, a movement in the corner of my eye caught my attention. I spun towards it, casting the armload of wood to the ground and raising my fists. But it was only the young witch, standing on the porch blinking at me blearily in the bright sunlight, her nipples stabbing like thumbtacks at the thin fabric of her undershirt.

For a moment, neither of us spoke. I would have tried to recover my dignity, pretend she hadn't caught me off guard, but it was too late for that. Instead, I swallowed, my eyes refusing to leave her tits. Finally, I broke the spell by kneeling to retrieve the scattered wood.

"You scared the shit out of me," I said, tossing the pieces into my free arm until my muscle strained under the weight. What was I thinking? I shouldn't even be looking at anyone else, not with Violet at the mercy of her kidnapper. Enduring god-only-knew what, probably at the hands of some pervert a hundred times worse than my darkest desires. And here I was, ogling some sweet little witch who had no idea what she was in for.

"You scared me," she accused, narrowing her blue eyes at me. "I woke up and you were gone. I thought you skipped out on me."

As guilt washed through me, I cursed myself on a hundred different levels. I should have taken the chance when she was sleeping, gotten the hell out of dodge. This chick may have been as naïve and blind as her grandmother believed, but she was plenty powerful, whether she knew it or not. From the look on her face, she wasn't going to let me out of her sight until her grandmother was safe and sound in the little cottage again.

And how could I say no? I knew what it was to lose someone, never knowing what had happened to them. No matter what happened, I wouldn't do that to her. No matter how her grandmother's words echoed in my head.

Bring my granddaughter to me. Deliver her at the eclipse.

Despite the chaos in my mind as I'd raced through the possibilities and worst-case scenarios, I'd had enough brain cells left to ask the obvious question. What if she didn't want to go? Why would she trust me?

The witch had assured me that her granddaughter would trust anyone. And if she didn't, she was certain I could think of some way to change her mind. And now here I was, stuck on this insane mission with yet another witch. And I couldn't just throw a sack over her head and haul her down the mountain, no matter what her grandmother had meant by her words.

She doesn't have much magic. That's what the lying old bag had promised. *She doesn't even know how to use most of it.*

But I'd nearly been a victim of her flame-throwing when I'd followed her through the woods the night before, and I hadn't gotten so lucky with her earth magic. She had plenty of magic, and she seemed adept at using it.

I'd known better than to believe the old crone, but I'd done it anyway, like the fool I was. At the end of the day, it didn't matter, though. Even if I'd known she was lying through her teeth, I would have agreed to her demands. I would have cut off my own hand if it would bring Violet back.

And it wasn't as if I were kidnapping Cayenne. I had a feeling that if I tried to leave right now, she'd probably kidnap me and force me to go along with her. What was the harm, anyway? She'd be reunited with her grandmother, and we'd all live happily ever after.

Chapter Eleven

Cayenne

I'd woken with a start, my undershirt sticking to me and my heart hammering. An urgency gripped me before I came fully awake. When I did, I'd cursed myself for sleeping so late. Mom always joked that if a nuclear bomb went off in the morning, I wouldn't find out until noon. But it wasn't funny this time. Tonight was the eclipse, and I needed to be up and in the wolves' valley by now.

I sat up, only to find Oral snoozing quietly beside me. The night before came crashing back with a throb of pain in my temples, and I winced, grabbing my head. Too many beers or too much excitement?

"Hey, girl," Oral said with a sleepy smile, his eyes fluttering open. He looked so sweet and peaceful in the sunlight streaming through the window, his hair all tousled and sexy. I ran a hand through my tangled mane, wondering how it was fair that he could look so perfect when he'd just woken up.

Not what you should be worrying about.

"I better get up," I said, swinging my legs off the bed.

Oral's arm circled my waist, and he sat up, nuzzling the back of my neck. "Hey," he said, a smile shining through his words. "Don't run out on me yet. I spent a whole night in bed with you and didn't even get a chance to show you my skills. You can't leave thinking I'm a loser."

I smiled and twisted towards him. "I don't think you're a loser," I said, holding his face between my hands. "I think you're a gentleman."

He scoffed. "I'd rather you think I was a scoundrel."

"What makes you think you can't be both?" I asked, leaning forward to plant a kiss on his lips. With that, I released him and hopped up from the bed. Oral groaned and threw himself backwards onto the bed as I slipped out the door, a grin on my face.

Guilt rushed into me when I saw the empty living room with the blankets rumpled on the couch. My heart lurched, and I thought I'd be sick. Had Efrain run out on me? I shouldn't be teasing boys who looked at me with such clear longing it made my thighs tremble, no matter how exciting and fun it was. I should be finding my grandmother with the help of the only shifter in the house who wasn't interested in me.

Outside, I heard a steady thump, and I raced out the back door. Efrain was stacking row upon row of firewood in the nearly empty woodshed. From the looks of it, he'd been at it for hours, maybe all night. But then I took stock of his bulging, tattooed biceps and decided that maybe he just worked a lot faster than me and my sisters.

For a moment, we stood taking measure of each other. I could see the appreciation in his eyes as they worked their way over me, and it made me want to strut like a peacock. I was busy taking him in, too—his broad shoulders, his arms, his strong, tattooed hands. His face wasn't classically handsome like Malik's. His dark hair bristled up in thick tufts, and his nose was a bit crooked as if it had been broken at some point. A scar bit into his upper lip, and his cheekbones and jaw were so chiseled they were almost harsh. But somehow, all put together, it worked. He looked rough and fierce, and he was looking at me like an animal watching his prey.

I quivered with a feeling that was foreign to me, an ache of longing buried deep inside me.

"Well, what are we waiting for?" I asked, the memory of the night before pressing down on me at full force. "Let's get going."

"I was just waiting for you to rise and shine, Sleeping Beauty," he drawled. I'd forgotten how deep and rough his voice was, almost a growl even as his lips twisted into a knowing smirk. As his eyes fixed on me, I had the feeling he knew exactly what I'd been thinking, as if he could feel my exact emotions through a bond of shared magic. But of course that was impossible. Even witches who shared my magic couldn't read my mind, though if I'd shared enough magic, they could sense my emotions.

But Efrain was a pig, not a warlock. He couldn't possibly sense the churn of desire and uncertainty, guilt and fear, warring inside my body, even though I'd given him healing magic. Mom had warned me about sharing magic with another person, how it could bind you to that person forever. That's how my parents had met. They'd encouraged me not to use magic with another person unless I was already attached, because it could form a bond between us.

That hadn't happened, though. If it had, I wouldn't find Efrain's smirk so infuriating.

"I'll get changed and then we can go," he said, slamming his ax down into a stump. The blade wedged there, halfway buried in the wood, the handle angled upwards. Efrain peeled off his shirt, steam rising from his sweaty, muscled body. His washboard abs glistened with moisture, the mosaic of tattoos across him fascinating in their complexity. I wanted to stand there longer, to trace my fingers over their lines, to decipher them like hieroglyphics.

Efrain pushed past me and strode into the house, leaving me standing on the porch, shaken. What had I done? Was this the result of the magic, or just plain lust? I'd never experienced either, so how would I know?

That isn't true, I told myself as I turned and entered the house. I had practiced healing on plenty of witches, including Malik. Which meant this was just an animal urge. An animal urge that was distracting me to a dangerous level.

*

"What are you laughing at?" Efrain growled when he emerged from the bedroom. He was wearing a backpack, which looked comically tiny on his huge frame.

"Nothing," I said, biting back a smile. "Heading off to school?"

"Either carry it yourself or shut up."

"Shutting up," I said, making a zipper motion across my lips.

Efrain took a menacing step towards me, and my breath caught. He didn't look like he meant to hurt me. He looked like he could barely contain himself from devouring me.

"You sure you don't need a third person for a stakeout?" Oral asked, interrupting our moment. "Or for entertainment?"

"I told you, the more people sneaking into the valley, the more likely we'll get caught," Efrain said.

Nelson frowned at the dishes he was washing, but he didn't say anything. He'd been quiet and grumpy all morning, and as much as I wanted to ask why or confront him about the night before, I didn't even know the guy. I wasn't shy, but this was just plain awkward. Leaving the house was a bit of a relief. There was too much tension crackling in the air between us, and something else between me and Oral. Altogether, it was just unsettling.

Despite what I'd thought about Efrain, and despite my attraction to him, he was somehow safer than the other two. He had a girlfriend, so there was no chance of anything messy happening between us, no matter what animal urges he'd awakened in me.

As we set off up the mountain at a brisk pace, Efrain striding ahead on his long legs, my questions came tumbling out. "What if…what if Granny is hurt? How are we going to carry her back?"

"I'll shift into a horse and you can ride me," he said with a smirk.

"Okay," I said, my pulse quickening at the reminder of the sensations I'd had the day before. Knowing it was him had made horseback riding a whole different experience.

"You liked that, huh?" Efrain said, his smile growing wider. Again, I noticed the gap where he was missing a tooth behind his canine. This time, I wondered how it would feel if we were kissing.

"It's efficient," I said lightly. "Where are we going now?"

"Over the river and through the woods," he said. "Any more burning questions?"

"Did you carry that backpack to school?"

"Yeah," he said. "Why?"

"No reason," I said. "Just curious. Did you go to shifter school?"

He snorted. "Shifters don't need training on how to shift. It comes naturally."

"But that's all the magic you have, right?" I asked, a little smug. Sure, I had to go to school for ages to learn all the different elements and spells, to learn about my familiar, herbology, and the history of witches and witchcraft. But there was a lot I could do once I learned it. All he could do was turn into a different animal.

"More useful than snapping your fingers to light a fire," he grumbled.

"You're right," I said quickly. I didn't want to argue or insult his people. I was just curious. "What did you go to school for, then?"

"The usual," he said. "Math, reading, science, all that bullshit."

"Where's the shifter school?"

He cast a strange look at me. "There's no shifter school," he said. "We go to school in Kingston."

"With regular humans?" I asked, turning so abruptly that my toe caught in a root and I pitched forward.

Efrain caught me so quickly that the blast of air I'd automatically raised to do the job slammed into us both. We stumbled back, Efrain's arms tightening protectively around me. "What the hell was that?"

"Sorry," I muttered. "Overreaction."

He looked down at me, his face guarded. "How much magic does that take?"

"Not much," I said, pulling away.

"How can you tell?" he asked as we began walking again.

"I just feel it," I said with a shrug.

"So, no one else knows how much magic you have," he said. "Only you can tell. You could trick someone into thinking you had a lot when really you weren't very powerful, and vice versa."

"If they'd take your word for it," I said. "It's not like you can stick a magical tire gauge on me and see if I'm running low. Witches can compete against each other to do the same tasks involving magic, so we all know who's strongest in our valley. And we can measure our capacity. But it's not a set amount. It shifts depending with use, practice, what you've been doing lately…"

Efrain frowned but didn't answer, seeming to mull that over for a few minutes.

"So, about this school…" I said when things had gotten too quiet for too long.

"What about it?" he asked, his voice edged with resentment. "It's not like I have no control over my shifting. I can fit in with humans as well as you."

"I probably can't fit in with humans at all," I said. "I've never been around them for more than a few hours when we go into town."

"Never?" he asked, looking at me askance. "They live all over our valley. All you have to do is cross the mountain from your valley into ours."

"I'm not allowed to," I admitted.

"I thought you were a big girl now," he said in a mocking tone.

"I am," I protested. "But it's not safe out there. People aren't safe out there. They never burned shifters at the stake, did they?"

Efrain snorted in response.

"It's true," I said. "My grandma lost all her magic because she left our valley."

Efrain frowned at me, hooking his thumbs in the straps of his comically small backpack. "You're right," he said after a minute. "It's not safe for you out here. You can't trust people of any nature. We're all shady. Not just shifty shifters."

I thought about all the times my parents had told me that if I saw anyone in our valley, I was supposed to run home and tell them, not even talk to the person. No shifters. No wolves. No one but witches and the others supernaturals in our coven could be trusted.

And yet, it was a warlock who had taken my grandmother's magic, who had made my parents so paranoid to begin with. In the thirty years since they'd fought the big bad warlock, a lot had changed. Maybe it was time to do away with those old fashioned notions and prejudices. If nothing else, shifters were tons of fun. I couldn't remember having this much excitement in my entire life. If not for the fact that Granny Golden had been taken captive, it would have been the adventure of a lifetime—sneaking into the wolf valley, flirting with sexy shifters around a bonfire…

"I don't think you're shifty," I said, striding to keep up with Efrain. "I think you're just what's been missing from my life."

Efrain snorted like a boar. "What are you on?"

"I'm on an adventure," I said, twirling around and spreading my arms. "That's what I've been missing. Don't get me wrong, the First Valley is home, and it's beautiful and safe, but…I want fun and adventure. I want danger and excitement and magic."

"Looks like you're going to get your wish," Efrain said, dropping his backpack.

My familiar swooped overhead, calling out in agitation. I pulled him closer, winding my magic tight inside.

Efrain grabbed his white T-shirt and ripped it straight down the middle, tossing the shredded material aside. His muscles rippled across his chest and abs, a snake tattoo curling up his ribs and across his chest, where a ferocious boar's head snarled out at me.

Momentarily struck dumb by his muscles, I stood there admiring him for a full ten seconds before his words registered. Just as they did, he grabbed me, thrusting my body behind his before the protest could leave my lips.

"What is it?" I asked, my eyes darting around the woods. It irked me a bit that he could sense something I couldn't.

He didn't have to answer. I caught movement in the corner of my vision and whipped my head around. A shadow slipped between the newly-budding trees, and a shiver raced down my spine. Another shadow caught my attention, and I spun to press my back against the solid wall of muscle that was Efrain.

I probably should not have noticed in that moment how incredibly huge his body felt against mine. But I did.

Just as quickly as the thought arose, it was replaced by the more pressing matter at hand.

Efrain muttered the word just as the first of them materialized.

"Wolves."

Chapter Twelve

Nelson

I couldn't stop thinking about Cayenne as I cleaned up the dishes. In the stories we heard in school and around the shifter community, witches were warty old ladies. But they had to start somewhere, I supposed.

I was pulled from my thoughts by a knock at the door. The hair along my neck stood up and I froze for a second, my hands still in the dishwater, my nostrils flaring. The smell of dish soap masked anything else, but I could hear the tap of high heels on the stones outside the doorway.

"Who's out there?" I asked, swiping a towel across my hands before heading for the front door. No one in the valley came knocking on my door unless they were looking for trouble.

"Come out, come out, wherever you are," sang a warbling voice. A voice I didn't know.

It wasn't some asshole coming to pick a fight because I'd pleased his wife so well she didn't need him anymore. Which meant it was some jilted lover coming to claim that I'd knocked her up and owed her big time.

"Who are you, and what do you want?" I asked.

"Let me come in," she said. I didn't recognize her voice, but that didn't mean much. I wasn't in the habit of remembering women for longer than one night.

"Like hell," I snarled, picking up my shotgun. "Not until you tell me what you want."

"I want my daughter," she said, still in that sing-song voice.

"Your daughter?" I said, pushing aside the curtain on the window beside the door. I held it back with the muzzle of the shotgun and took in the lady on my porch. She looked more like a woman I would have taken home than one whose daughter I'd banged. Maybe she was a few years older than us, but not too old. The curves and shiny blonde hair didn't hurt any.

"Yes, my daughter," she snapped. "The witch you're delivering to me."

She looked nothing like Cayenne, but they were both hot, so I guessed I had her to thank for Cayenne's bewitching us all.

"Your daughter's not here," I said.

"I think she is," she said. "Send her out, or I'll use air magic and knock your door right down."

"What's going on?" Oral asked, strolling into the room.

"Apparently Cayenne's mom is here for her," I said. "We should have known we'd get burned if we let something that hot into our home."

Oral scratched the back of his head and grinned. "She was pretty hot, wasn't she?"

"You leave me no choice," the old witch said, tottering backwards across the yard in her high heels.

"What the hell is she doing?" Oral asked, joining me at the window.

"She's trying to blow the door down," I said. "We should have known her coven would come fetch her. How could we be so stupid?"

"Maybe she enchanted us," Oral said. "Not our fault."

"I know an excuse when I hear one," I growled. "She told us up front she'd run away. Of course the coven's going to come after her."

"Don't blame yourself," Oral said, clapping me on the shoulder. "Our judgment was clouded by the hot girl in our midst. We can't be held accountable."

The witch outside was swirling her hands and chanting, conjuring up some magic.

"Think this old house'll hold?" Oral asked.

"It better," I said, but in truth, I just didn't know. I wasn't a warlock, I was a boar. I didn't know anything about magic other than what our granddaddy had told us. I'd stayed in the valley, worked hard and fought harder to keep what our father had given me. Efrain was the one who had gone off after Violet and experienced the world on his way. When it came right down to it, I was as sheltered as that little witch.

But Dad had left me more than a good solid foundation to start my life. He'd left me the protection charm granddaddy had gotten from a witch before I was born, one that blocked all magic. As long as it was in the house, it couldn't be destroyed by anything the witch threw at it.

A blast of wind hit the house so hard the window rattled in its frame. The curtain blew back in the draft, and dust and pebbles pelted the front of the house.

The witch shrieked in fury, her pretty face turning purple as she stamped her foot. "Send her out," she screeched.

"That ain't much of a negotiation," Oral said. He cracked the window and leaned down to call out to her. "What do you want with her?"

"She's set to marry the wolf king, and nothing you can do will stop it," the witch howled. "I should have known you shifty shifters couldn't be trusted to get the job done. What has she said to convince you to shelter her? Did she mewl about what a terrible mother I am, forcing her to marry a man she doesn't know? It's all lies! This is her destiny! She can't escape it."

With a burst of magic, the witch hurled debris against the front of our house. They thumped against the stones of the house, which trembled slightly as the rocks rained down to the ground around it.

I shared a look with Oral. It seemed there was a lot Cayenne had failed to mention in her short time here. "Why would you force your daughter to marry a man she doesn't know?" Oral asked the witch.

No wonder she'd run away.

"Do you not understand the word destiny?" the witch asked, muttering to herself. "I should have known. My own daughter is a shifty shifter in her nature, isn't she?"

"I thought she was a witch," I said.

"She can be both," the witch snapped, turning her attention back to us. "Didn't she tell you? I thought that's how she'd gained your trust. She must have offered something else. What is it? Oh, you shifters are such animals that she probably only had to offer you her virgin body in return for your protection. Is that it?" She sneered horribly, her face twisting into something hideous. "Did you take turns with her, or has only one of you ravaged her innocence?"

"Fuck off, old hag," Oral said. "We're never giving her up."

With a scream of rage, the witch shot flames from her palms, bathing the front of the house. I jumped back from the window, dropping the curtain. To think I'd been impressed by Cayenne's little spark that lit the bonfire the night before. This witch had just sent a wall of flame up the front of our house.

Luckily, we weren't in my brother's little tinderbox trailer, or we'd have been toast.

"An enchantment," she howled in outrage. "Who put a protection spell on this house? How dare they protect a shifter from my powers? My daughter couldn't have done this with her puny magic, so who else are you harboring?"

"I think you'd better go," I said, nudging the curtain aside with my shotgun again. "You're not going to get what you want here."

"I'll be back," she raged. "You'll regret this. Mark my words, you filthy stinking pigs."

With that, she turned and marched off across the yard. We waited until she disappeared from view to speak. "Think she's right?" Oral asked.

"I already regret it," I said. "But that won't stop me from doing what I'm about to do."

"What if she really does come after us?" Oral asked.

"We'll have to take the protection charm with us," I said. "Now, let's go warn them."

Chapter Thirteen

Cayenne

I expected Efrain to change into a boar, but before he could, one of the wolves changed into a man. Even though I'd seen tons of naked guys in my life, my eyes still had the embarrassing tendency to wander south. The middle-aged Hispanic guy in front of us ignored my perusal. "We have warned you to stop invading our valley," he said, his voice hard and clear. "Your constant trespassing will not be tolerated under our new leader."

"We just want my grandma back," I said, holding up both hands. "We're not here to invade. We brought no army."

"I don't know anything about your grandmother," the man said. "We have only wolves in or valley. And we're tired of you shifters crossing our boundaries as if they don't exist, taking from our valley because you depleted your own."

As he spoke, I realized that he thought I was a shifter. The thought made me want to laugh, but not in the horrified way my parents would have. I didn't mind that he thought I was a shifter. It was not offensive or insulting now that I knew them. I liked shifters.

Wolves, not so much.

I wanted my granny back, and this lying dog was not going to keep me from getting her.

"You sure you ain't seen her granny?" Efrain asked, sounding amused. "Old lady, grey hair, about yay high?" He held up a hand to show how tall she was.

"No," the wolf-man said, grinding his teeth. "Now get out of our valley. We won't tell you again."

"You sure-sure?" Efrain asked. "No old Chinese lady wandered by lately? Because I might have seen her here with my own eyes."

"She's not Chinese," I hissed. "Those are wrinkles around her eyes."

"Whatever," Efrain said with a shrug. "I don't think these dogs are going to obey. Which means we might have to fight."

Without warning, his body exploded into a huge, spiny boar. He charged straight for the man, but before he could reach him, the other two wolves, who had stayed in wolf form, leapt into his way. Efrain's tusk gouged into one of the wolves, and I bit back a horrified scream as a bloody, crimson gasp appeared in the wolf's grey pelt.

I'd wanted excitement, not violence. Of course, I had trained for fighting, but now that an attack was actually happening, I froze. I didn't want to hurt anyone. Witches fought with shields and magic, clean and neat. There was no blood in a witch fight.

Wolves and shifters fought dirty. The wolves were snarling, leaping in to bite at Efrain as he charged one way and another, trying to skewer another wolf. Even the one he'd hit was still standing, snapping when he came near. The others were protecting it, I realized, drawing Efrain away.

And I was standing there, useless as an ordinary human.

Do something, I screamed at myself. Robin swooped overhead, chirping in agitation.

I raised my hands to do something my parents had told me never to do—use magic to hurt someone. Robin cheeped even louder, and I could feel his disapproval. But this was self-defense. Or at least defense of a friend.

I tossed a fireball at one of the wolves, who tumbled into the leaves with an agonized howl. Instantly, something dark coiled through me, invading my magic. I tried to push it out, but I couldn't. After a second, I realized it was the magic itself, turning dark.

The last wolf took that moment to seize Efrain by the throat. With a hideous shriek, he bucked to shake the wolf loose, but it held on.

To hell with the rules. I could heal my magic later. I lifted my hands, trying to find an opening that would ensure I hit the wolf and not Efrain. Before I found it, two giant boars thundered past me. One of them hit the wolf who had clamped down on Efrain's throat, and it came loose, flying through the air and smacking into a tree trunk. The other boar charged straight for the wolf I'd hit with the fireball. Before he got there, the wolf leapt to its feet and streaked off through the woods.

The boars were impressive and quick, but the wolves were quicker. Even the one that Efrain had gouged jumped up and ran to the one who had hit the tree. With a furious roar, the three boars charged again. The wolf leapt out of the way, snapping at them for a moment before seeing it was hopelessly outnumbered. It turned and fled, leaving a mournful howl trailing behind as the three boars descended on the last wolf.

I tried not to look. I didn't want to look, but I couldn't tear my eyes away as their tusks ripped through fur skin and flesh. The wolf howled and snarled and screamed, but it was buried under their tearing teeth and slicing tusks. Sickness swept over me, and I hugged my arms around my belly, fighting for control. A sob gripped my throat, and Robin landed on my shoulder, trying in vain to comfort me.

A minute later, the boars retreated, bloody and victorious. They circled the wolf's remains, then lifted their snouts and scented the air before turning back to human. They started high-fiving each other and laughing about their great moments, even though blood was still running out of Efrain's throat, down his chest.

Finally, they seemed to remember I was there.

"Nice job, little witch," Oral said, throwing an arm around my neck. He smelled like sweat and animal, a strong and heady scent that wasn't exactly unpleasant. The smell of blood was what turned my stomach.

I threw his arm off and spun on them. "You killed that wolf!" I said, my voice more hysterical than I wanted.

"Of course we killed it," Efrain said, gesturing to his neck. "It would have killed us."

"You didn't have to kill it," I said, drawing a shaky breath. "You could have let it run off. They know we're here now, anyway. They're going to go home and tell the others."

"She's right about that," Nelson said. "We should get out of wolf territory quick. They'll all know he's dead by now, anyway, through their pack bond."

"Pack bond?" I asked, still sounding slightly unhinged. "Do you have that?"

"No," Nelson said.

I'd heard of the bond, but it seemed somehow human to me, a way to telepathically communicate while in wolf form. But they weren't human. They were all animals.

Suddenly, I missed Malik with painful intensity. His safe arms, his easy smile, his simple dreams that included a peaceful family. These men danced with death as if it were a familiar face.

Efrain picked up his tattered shirt and wrapped it around his neck like a bandage. "You'll have to fix me up good when we get out of wolf territory."

I swallowed hard, wondering if my magic would even work now. It had been tainted, and now that I was so shaken, I didn't know if I could heal him at all. That took love, and I was slightly horrified by all of them now.

I just wanted to curl up in Malik's safe arms and know that someone would understand how appalled I was at the violence I'd witnessed. That wasn't an option right now, but I vowed I would marry that boy the day I got back to our valley. I wanted adventure, but I wanted the familiarity of home, too.

"I can see you're upset," Nelson said, approaching me. He stopped without trying to touch me and stood before me, naked and bloody. "This is the way it is for us. We're animals. Not some great and noble beasts. Nature isn't majestic. It's brutal. If we hadn't killed that wolf, they would have killed us. It's that simple."

"You could have made peace," I muttered.

"There hasn't been peace between the valleys for decades."

I knew he was right. My parents had warned me about this, the warring neighbors in the other valleys. But it hadn't sunk in until now. I fought a wave of nausea when I thought of that wolf screaming as they sliced it apart and left it there like worthless bones. I'd known these guys were shifters, had even seen them in animal form. I'd just never realized that they were really animals, that their natures, their moral code, was so inhuman.

Chapter Fourteen

Cayenne

"We need to get out of the wolves' valley," Efrain said. "Now that we've gotten one of theirs, they'll send the whole pack for us. And we can't fight the whole pack."

"What about my grandma?" I asked. "While you're busy killing each other, she's still down there. If you want to fight the whole pack, maybe I can sneak down while they're busy and find her."

"We don't want to fight the whole pack," Efrain said. "That's what I'm saying. So let's go."

"No," I said planting my feet. "You said we'd come get my grandma out. And instead, you had to go murdering each other. But that's not part of my plan. My plan is to get my grandma."

"Then I hope you're planning to die," he said. "Because they're pissed now."

"That's not my fault," I said. To my horror, my eyes started to ache with tears. Sure, last night had been fun, but today was serious. I needed Granny Golden back. The violence, leaving the valley without even attempting to find her—this wasn't supposed to happen.

Efrain's voice came in a soft rumble this time. "Like I said, sometimes the bravest thing to do is run," he said. "We don't have much time, Cayenne. We'll go back tonight and get her."

"When she's already dead?" I asked, more furious that he was speaking gently to me, like he knew I was about to cry.

Nelson raised his head and sniffed the air. "He's right," he said. "We gotta get out of here."

"She'll be alive tonight," Efrain said, his lips tightening into a grim line. "They'll make sure of it."

"I'll give you a lift," Oral said quietly, stepping up beside me. His warm hand closed over mine, and he gave it a gentle squeeze. "We're not going to leave you here to die when the wolves come."

I nodded, my throat too tight to speak.

"What do you like to ride?" he asked, a twinkle in his eye.

I tried to answer, forcing the knot from my throat.

"She's good on a horse," Efrain said, and he shifted into a stallion before I could answer.

"A horse is good," I said.

Nelson shifted into the huge boar I'd ridden the night before. Oral crouched, and I could see him straining. He didn't shift as smoothly as the others—at least not this time. Now I understood why Efrain had bragged about the ease with which he could shift. Oral's head jerked back and forth as he lurched a step forward.

Efrain nudged me with his big head. And even though I'd hugged on it before, that was only because I liked horses. Not because I liked him. I shoved his head away.

He snorted and pricked his ears. Distantly, I heard a howl down in the valley.

"Whatever," I said. "I'll ride a boar. Just shift, already."

Oral shook his head, his eyes squeezed closed and his face turning red. Fur rippled along his arms. Nelson nudged me with his nose, then turned his head back, motioning for me to get on.

"I got it," Oral grunted.

Another minute passed, and I heard the howls again. This time, they sounded much closer. I turned to Nelson, but before I could climb on, something tugged at my cloak. When I turned back, a small horse grey stood there grinning at me.

"You did it," I said, smiling despite myself. "Pretty much, anyway."

Nelson snorted, and even though he was a boar, I was pretty sure he was laughing.

I petted Oral's head, which was shorter than Efrain's, and his long, droopy ears. "These are some big ears."

He nipped at my dress, tugging on the sleeve this time.

"And some pretty big teeth," I said, regarding him again.

He lowered his head, and I grabbed on and tried to mount him. Even though his back was really low, I couldn't manage it. I threw my leg up, but it only hit his back. I tried again, gripping the fur below his mane and throwing my leg as high as I could. A ripping sound happened somewhere in the posterior of my dress.

Shit, how did people do this? I tried to mount headfirst this time, gripping on with both hands and dragging myself up. I got my chest and shoulders on, then threw my leg up. Just then, Efrain decided to help me out by nudging my bottom with his big nose, and quite thoroughly, I might add. He burrowed his muzzle deep between my thighs and pushed.

"Get off my butt," I said, swatting at him. I heaved myself up so hard that I lost my balance and started to slide over the opposite side of Oral's back.

This was plain silly. Here was the most powerful young witch in the valley, flailing around in a completely undignified manner, trying to mount a donkey while a horse molested her. A little magic would not be wasted here.

I brought up a blast of air in time to keep my body from tumbling to the ground on the far side of Oral like a sack of oats. I scrambled upright and buried my hands in his short mane. Then I smacked Efrain's side with a small stone just for fun.

He whinnied and bit at my boot, but I gave him a swift kick. Oral must have thought that was for him, because he bolted forward. I threw myself flat and clung to him with arms and legs—and a little more magic. We headed up the mountain Efrain had led me down, leaves and rocks tumbling under their feet and bare branches snagging at my face. I put my head down, breathing in Oral's animal smell. He smelled like a donkey when he was in donkey form, which was comforting. After all the craziness and horror of the day, something familiar and safe was a welcome change.

They stopped at a tiny wooden shack in the woods not far over the mountain from wolf territory.

"Is this safe?" I asked as I slid off Oral's back. He immediately shifted back into his human form, letting out a sigh of relief when he was there. The other two shifted easily as well.

"Dude, your horse was such an epic fail," Efrain said, slugging Oral's shoulder.

"A donkey, man, you were a donkey," Nelson said, shoving him.

Oral laughed along with them, shoving them back, but his face went bright red.

"Is this place safe?" I asked again, interrupting their horseplay. "We're not very far from the wolves."

"They're scared of us," Efrain said, smearing blood across his broad chest as he wiped at a drop trickling between his bulging pectorals.

I bit my lip, trying not to stare. I should be disgusted. But…

Damn it, why did I use healing magic on him?

"They don't leave their territory," Nelson said. "They'll attack if we cross into their valley, but they won't cross the border into ours."

"They know we'll show no mercy," Efrain said, his chest swelling with pride.

"You're a savage, you know that?" I said.

"I've been told it's my best quality." He swiped more blood off his chest and took a step closer. "You wanna fix us up, Little Red? As much as I enjoy standing around gossiping, I'm losing a lot of blood here."

"Will you show mercy on me?" I asked, crossing my arms.

"Not even if you beg," Efrain said with a smirk.

I glanced at the decrepit shack, wondering who used it. Hopefully someone with clothes. I didn't really like being alone in the woods with three naked men who lacked basic human morals. I had magic to protect myself, of course, but I was more worried about what they might make me *want* to do.

My familiar stirred uneasily, sensing my discomfort.

"Then no healing magic," I said, tossing my head. My red curls spilled over my shoulders and my velvet cloak.

"He's joking," Oral said, his fingers grazing my arm. "We ain't gonna hurt you. We know not to cross a witch."

"I need a promise," I said.

"I promise," he said, his blue eyes kind and serious for once. "We can hang out at this old hunting cabin for the day, and go back in tonight, when they're busy with the eclipse."

"I'm going to go lie down," Efrain said, his face looking a little pale. "It'll give us a little privacy." He winked, but it was half-hearted. He was really bloody. I sighed and turned to follow him as he stumbled inside. I heard the creak of metal springs that sounded like a cot protesting its use.

"Your mother came looking for you," Nelson said behind me.

"What?" I whirled around, my legs twisting up in my skirt. "My mom?"

"Yeah," he said. "She's a piece of work. I can see why you ran away."

"I didn't run away," I said. "And my mom is amazing."

"She sure is," he said. "She firebombed my house."

I blinked stupidly at him, thinking of his solid stone house that had kept the wolves at bay all night. "What?"

"Don't worry, it had a charm on it," he said. "That's how I knew we'd be safe there last night. But she was not happy about that."

"Or the fact that we wouldn't hand you over," Oral said. "Not that we could. You'd already gone."

"Lucky we had that charm, or we'd be barbecue right now."

"My mom would never…" I trailed off. My mom totally would. She'd do anything for me, and she had a temper like mine. If she thought they were holding me hostage? All bets were off.

"You'd better go help Efrain," Oral said, touching a small cut above his hip. "And if you wouldn't mind patching me up afterwards…"

Great. More forbidden healing magic.

I was going to be in so much trouble when I got home.

Chapter Fifteen

Cayenne

The little shack was a small room with only a couple windows, which made it seem even smaller and gloomier. I left the door open to let some light in as I approached the cot. I sat down on the edge, in the tiny sliver of space left next to Efrain's hip. "How come you're always the one having a near-death experience?" I asked.

"Would you rather one of my brothers had gotten hurt?" he asked. "I wouldn't."

"I'd really rather not have a closer bond with you than I already have."

"That's worn off," Efrain said. "Didn't you notice? We're back to fighting."

Was he right? I sat with my magic, trying to feel it. I could still feel the dark tendrils in it, like wisps of smoke. That was bad enough. Besides that, though, the fact that Efrain had noticed the change in our bond before I had unsettled me. But what unsettled me more was that not only was the magic gone, but I still felt something other than mutual distrust, disgust, and irritation.

"Don't put your spell on me again," he said. "I'd rather die than think I love a witch."

"You thought you loved me?"

"You stopped frustrating the hell out of me," he said. "That's pretty much the same thing, right?"

"But that's all gone?" I asked.

"Every last bit."

That made sense. Most humans didn't have a capacity for magic. We could use it on them, and it would enter them for a short time, but it drained away. They couldn't gather it, hold it inside, and use it like a witch. I'd healed Efrain, and my magic had entered him, but it hadn't stayed inside him. Which meant my feelings probably had nothing to do with the magic. I was just plain attracted to this bloody beast.

"You still saved my life when I froze up in the woods," I said, touching his cheek.

"Yeah, well, I don't make a habit of watching little girls get eaten by wolves."

"And I don't make a habit of watching men bleed to death like stuck pigs." His shoulders were already spilling off the edges of the cot, so I had no choice but to lay down on his chest, shaking my curls back so they'd spill over the side of the bed instead of onto his bloody skin. By turning sideways, I managed to squeeze my hips and legs onto the bed beside him.

Efrain groaned, his arm circling me and pressing me closer to his bare body.

"We usually slit their throats so they'll go quickly," I said. "When we kill pigs, I mean."

"You're one twisted little witch," he said.

"You're one naked, big man," I whispered, keenly aware of the heat of his skin burning through my dress.

"You say that like it's a bad thing."

"Promise you won't take advantage of whatever I'm feeling after I share magic with you," I said, my fingers tightening in his tufts of dark hair.

"But that's what I do best."

"Promise, or I'm not healing you."

"Maybe you should be promising that," he said. "It's your magic. What if you take advantage of me?"

"I'm serious," I said, tugging on his hair again. "I—I've never…"

I didn't know why I couldn't say it. Everyone in my entire valley knew, and no one had ever cared. I had never cared. But suddenly, I did. It was just that they'd all joked about sex like men used to getting it.

A laugh rumbled through his chest. "You've gotta be kidding me."

"Sex is sacred to us," I said. "It's sacred to me. But obviously not to you. To you, nothing's sacred. Not even life."

I sat up and swung my legs off the edge of the bed.

Efrain's thick arm circled my waist. I knew I could get away using magic, but what scared me was that I was pretty sure I could get away without it. His grip was half-hearted, his strength fading. "I won't take advantage of you, Cayenne. I swear. Don't go. I…I need you."

When I turned back to him, his eyes had fallen closed. I lay back down beside him, hoping I hadn't waited too long. I wrapped my arms around him as I had the night before.

"You better still mean it when you're back to full strength," I whispered against his cheek. Stubble had grown out scratchy and rough on his cheeks, but when I pressed my cheek to his, it seemed to soften.

"First time for everything," Efrain muttered.

I closed my eyes and let my magic flow into him.

A few minutes later, Efrain opened his eyes and looked at me.

Oh no. I recognized that look from the night before. I couldn't believe I'd ever thought he wasn't handsome. His unconventional face was fascinating, beautiful. His hazel eyes shone with all the colors of a forest deep enough to get lost in.

"Hey, there, Little Red," he said, his arm tightening around me. In one movement that was so fluid it had to be practiced to an expert level, he rolled over, pulling me under him at the same time. "That's better."

It did feel better. It felt so much better, so right, to be crushed under this boulder of a man. I felt small and delicate, as if he could break my bones as easily as snapping a twig but would never dream of it. He would hold me in his big hands like a baby bird, treat me as gently.

His hands gripped the frame of the cot and his hips rolled on mine, crushing me harder into the thin mattress. I gasped, my body responding while my mind was still in a whirl. I arched up against him, and he groaned, grinding me deeper into the mattress.

With a squeal of metal, the cot gave way, the metal frame slamming down on the wood floor with a bang.

A high laugh burst from my mouth, and Efrain grinned. "Guess this bed's only made for one."

"Efrain, get off her, you heathen," Nelson said, grabbing Efrain's shoulders. He and Oral hauled Efrain up.

Oral offered a hand and pulled me up. "You all right?"

"I'm fine," I said, brushing at my skirt. My head was still spinning. Promise or no promise, I didn't like the way I felt after sharing love magic with Efrain. How out of control, as if my brain could no longer command my body, let alone my hormones.

On the bright side, healing him seemed to have cured the dark streak in my magic, too. Cleansing, healing, and love were all one kind of magic.

"Got any left for me?" Oral asked.

I sighed and gestured to the other cot. Besides the two cots, there wasn't much to the hunting shack, just a counter with a camping stove, a dish rack, and a sink with two gallon jugs of water beside it.

"You really stay here when you're hunting?" I asked.

"Sometimes," he said with a shrug. He lay on the edge of the cot, propped up on one elbow. "I'm not sure who it really belongs to. Maybe King Owen. But lots of folks use it."

"King Owen?"

"The shifter king," he explained.

"You have a for-real king?"

"Yeah, but he's kind of a joke," Oral said, patting the bed in front of him. "Want me to cuddle you like Efrain did?"

"It's not cuddling," I said, arranging myself on the edge of the bed. It was still a tight fit, but he didn't take up the entire bed. He had turned on his side to give me more space, but that required me to lie facing him. His eyelashes were long and dark, curling downwards as he watched my mouth.

"Whatever it is, I want some," he said, his voice low.

That same sense of power I'd felt before swelled inside me. After a lifetime of training with other witches, where power was only measured in the ability to do magical tasks, it was intoxicating. This was not magic, not the power of being a witch. Rather the power of being a woman.

It was a power built on contradictions. Though it was my own, these men had awakened it when they looked at me the way they had, wanting me. It was both exhilarating and terrifying, made me feel both powerful and helpless over it.

I lay my hand on Oral's side, letting magic flow into him. Now that I'd done it a few times, it had become easier.

Or maybe because you care about them more…

I wanted to deny that thought, but there was no getting around it. Even though I was now sure I could call Efrain a pig with no irony whatsoever, I had shared more than magic with him. We'd shared experiences, dangers, hurt and healing. Oral was sweet and funny, and he had held me through the night. And Nelson had shared his home with me, not to mention that moment I'd put aside for later consideration.

A shadow fell across the open door, and there he stood. Efrain still sat on the collapsed cot, and Oral lay beside me, his hand resting on my hip.

"Thank you," he said, a smile forming on his lips. "How about you let us show our thanks with a little gift of our own."

"What's that?" I asked. My mind immediately latched onto an idea, but I wasn't sure that's what they meant, so I tried to imagine something else they could give me when all they had was themselves.

"Let me show you," he said, tugging gently at the fabric of my skirt. "I call it… The gift of my namesake."

"And them?" I asked, my eyes meeting Nelson's.

"You're a greedy little thing, aren't you?" Efrain said with a smirk.

"That's not what—" I started to protest, my face flaming.

"I already gave you my word, so they'll have to be enough for today. Not as fun, is it?"

"I'm not going to do that with any of you," I said. "That's for the first member of my collective."

His face split into that wolfish grin. "Guess I'll have to watch and make sure they don't get out of line."

"They?" I asked, gulping.

Nelson's green eyes met mine, almost glowing with heat. "I was taught to always repay a favor," he said. "Especially to a witch."

"Since you're a witch, isn't this the norm for you?" Oral said. "Think of us as your collection for the day."

"Collective," I corrected, my voice faint. Of course he was right. My parents had several houses, and when they all went off to spend time together without the kids... I tried not to think about it.

But I had to face it now. I had three men practically begging for my favor. Nelson knelt beside me, his mouth claiming mine, his arms around me. Oral's hands and mouth took more liberties as they roamed over my body. As Nelson's kisses moved to my throat, Efrain stood over us, proudly exposed, as if wanting me to know exactly how much self-restraint it took to oversee without participating.

I reached for him, but he shook his head. "A promise is a promise," he said, his voice a low rumble in the tiny shack.

"I didn't make you promise not to touch me."

"No takebacks," he said. "And you're a greedy little witch. Have I said that enough yet?"

My attention was captured by Oral's hands on my bare skin, and I closed my eyes and let the sensations wash over me. There was no rule about this. I wasn't supposed to talk to shifters, but no one said anything about kissing them. And if there had been a rule against it, it wouldn't have mattered. If breaking rules felt this good, I was going to break every single one of them.

Chapter Sixteen

Efrain

We waited for evening, when the wolves would be deep in preparation for their monthly shift as well as the party for the eclipse. Their new king would take over then. All I had to do was deliver him a wife and my job would be done. I could go after Violet then.

As we made our way out of the hunting cabin, the last of the evening's pale, February sunlight slanted down on Cayenne, making her brick red hair shine. It lit up her fair skin and her smattering of freckles, making her look more like a nature faerie than a witch. I kept looking at her, trying to remember if Violet had been that naïve. Surely she hadn't. She'd never have followed me down this mountain, trusting that I'd help her. She'd have laughed and scratched the shit out of me and run off on her own. Violet didn't like my help. Actually, Violet really hadn't liked anything about me.

She wouldn't have come to rescue her granny, either. Violet was part witch, but she didn't have magic and said the witches didn't respect her. According to her, her granny was batshit crazy, and I couldn't disagree now that I'd met her.

Granny Golden. The name had startled me the first time it came from Cayenne's lips. I'd stopped trying to figure out how they had the same granny. They were cousins, that's how. So what and big deal. Everyone in the shifter valley was related, so why not this one, too? Maybe Cayenne would even be happy knowing she was doing this to save her cousin, too.

At last, we started down the final mountain towards the clearing where wolves did their ceremonies. Cayenne was silent. I didn't blame the chick. I wanted to puke, too. Had Violet ever blindly trusted me this way, even when we were kids and I might have been a decent guy? Even when we were grown, and I was decent for her?

I heard footsteps in the leaves, twigs snapping off to the left. My head jerked around.

"Someone's in the woods," Nelson said.

"I'll go," I said. "You stay here and guard Cayenne."

She rolled her eyes. Violet would have done that. But Cayenne didn't tell me to go fuck myself like Violet would have.

"I can guard us all," Cayenne said smugly. "I'll make a shield."

"Sounds good to me," said Oral.

"I'll go with you," Nelson said to me. "In case there's a group patrolling."

I cast a doubtful glance at Cayenne and Oral. Not that he wouldn't throw himself in front of a train to save a damsel who might be in his bed later, but he wasn't the best fighter among us.

"Come on," Nelson said, peeling off the hunting clothes we'd dug up in the cabin. He shifted into boar form and started off, scenting as he went.

I hesitated, torn between going out to scout for danger and staying to protect this crazy, trusting, innocent witch. But only because she was the key to finding Violet, I reminded myself.

"Take care of him," I said to Cayenne, nodding at Oral. "Don't let me come back to find him sliced up into pork chops."

"I will," she said, her voice soft, as if she knew I'd rather tell him to take care of her.

I turned away, stripped, and shifted into boar form, too. I hurried to catch up with Nelson, and we picked up our pace. People gave us shit for being pigs our whole lives, but that was just ignorant. Our tusks were deadly, our noses were as sharp as any wolf's, and we had the biggest dicks of any mammal. Just saying.

We arrived on an old trail that lead from the wolf community over the mountain into our territory. A minute later, we rounded a bend and came upon two women. Not wolves, not scouts. Human women.

I shifted back into human form, too. The younger girl screamed and jumped behind the old woman, using her as a shield. I immediately recognized both of them, and the sense of relief that went through me almost buckled my knees.

"You escaped," I said, not aiming my words at either one in particular.

"Where's my granddaughter?" the old woman asked. She was wearing army fatigues for some odd reason, as if that could disguise her from wolves and boars.

"She's safe," I said.

"If you don't deliver her as agreed upon, you'll see why they tell you never to cross a witch."

"I thought I was trading her for you."

"They'll still take her," the witch said. "If they know what's good for them. And you'll take her to them if you know what's good for you. After that little stunt you played today, I ought to turn you into a human torch."

"What are you talking about?" the girl asked. I knew her, too. She was a princess—our princess. King Owen's daughter, the one I'd tried to rescue from the wolves. Because of her, I'd been injured, and this batty old witch had saved me for the very purpose of gaining a favor from me. If not for her, I'd be dogfood for that pack back there. If not for both of them.

But I found it hard to bow down, even to royalty.

"Don't worry your pretty little mind," I said. "You're going to find Owen, right?"

"That's right," the old witch said. "And you're delivering my granddaughter to the wolves."

Nelson had shifted behind me, and now he spoke up. "Like hell," he said. "We ain't turning her over."

"You most certainly are," the witch said. "Or I'll fry you up like sausage and eat you myself."

"Listen, you old witch," Nelson said, stepping toward her.

"You're pretty close to earning a curse," the witch said. "Now give my daughter to her rightful husband, or you'll be sorry. She will be a queen there. What can you offer her? A side of bacon?"

Nelson scowled.

I owed this old bag my life, like it or not. "I'll try," I said. "But I think she's been holding out on you. She's got more magic than you think."

Granny laughed. "Too much for three little pigs to handle?" As quickly as it appeared, her smile vanished. Her eyes flashed. "Put a block on her." She reached out and snatched up a necklace the princess wore. "Like this. A charm that blocks her magic."

"Great idea," I said. "I guess any old rock will do? Or where do you expect me to get one of those?"

"You already have one," she said with a smirk.

"I do?"

"He does," she said, pointing a sharp fingernail at my brother.

I turned to him. "What the hell, man?"

He shrugged. "Grandpa passed it down with the house. It protects it."

"Hand it over," I said, holding out a hand.

"It's in the backpack," he said. "Back with Oral."

"Time draws near," the witch said, nodding up at the full moon that hung low and huge over the horizon. "Make haste. We'll meet again when the time is right."

"What if I can't do it," I called after the witch as she turned and started walking up the trail again.

"Then your family will be cursed," she said. "Your flower will die, and your home will be blown down by a gust of wind."

I cursed under my breath. Suddenly, strong hands grabbed and spun me around. My fists were up before I saw that it was just my brother.

"What the hell are you doing?" he demanded.

"She saved my life," I said. "She called in the favor."

His fingers crushed into my shoulders. "What are you doing to Cayenne?"

"I'm making her a princess," I said, jerking away. "The old lady's right. She wants a good marriage for her granddaughter. What can we give her?"

"She seemed pretty happy with what we gave her today."

"You think a king can't give her the same thing?"

"Wolves mate for life. Their king won't be happy knowing we touched his queen."

"You touched her," I said. "I never laid a finger on her."

"You bastard," he said, grabbing for me.

"Calm down," I said, holding him off. "No one will know. She's still a virgin for him, and she's smart enough not to tell him the other things she's done."

"You should have told us the whole plan."

"You knew I was repaying the witch."

"I didn't know you'd be throwing Cayenne to the wolves tonight."

"It's for the best," I said. "She'll get to live as royalty, I'll get Violet back, and every time you see their asshole king, you and Oral can know you've tasted his wife. Everyone wins."

"Violet?" he asked, his eyes narrowing. "All this is for Violet?" He grabbed my shoulders, shaking me hard. "When are you going to get it through your thick skull that Violet is the worst thing that ever happened to you? She never cared about you, man. I'm sorry to tell you that so bluntly, but you've got to let her go. She tried to tell you herself before she left. You were never anything but a high school fling to her, and you're wasting your life on her. She's not waiting for you to rescue her, Efrain. She doesn't want you to find her. She probably doesn't even remember your name."

I shoved him away, hard, and he went reeling back, knocking into a tree.

"You're wrong," I said. "When I find her, you'll see." I had to get away from him, far away, so he couldn't catch me and plant those poison barbs in my brain any more. I shifted into a cheetah and ran. But even I knew I was running from the truth.

Chapter Seventeen

Cayenne

At dark, we stopped a little ways from the clearing. We didn't want the wolves to scent us, even though they weren't yet in wolf form. We sat on a log and ate some deer jerky from Efrain's backpack. He and Nelson had apparently gotten into a fight, and they weren't speaking.

I didn't have time to worry about their squabbles. I was trying to make out my grandmother through the trees. The clearing had filled with wolves, or rather, their human counterparts. I had to put Robin in my hood, so he wouldn't go crazy, but he was still squirming with irritation, sensing my distress. Below, the wolves were chatting and eating under a pavilion like peaceful, civilized witches who would never dream of sacrificing a sacred life. They had families, kids and teenagers, including a super handsome boy with glossy black hair and a whole lot of swagger.

"That's the future king," Nelson said. "At the eclipse, he thinks he's taking over."

"We've got news for him," Oral said, rubbing his hands together gleefully.

Efrain frowned and studied the group. I did, too. Most of the adults were under the pavilion, and though I spotted an old lady or two, I couldn't find my granny anywhere among them.

"Where's Granny Golden?" I hissed.

"Maybe she already escaped," Nelson said.

"They're not going to let her hang out at their party and mingle," Efrain said.

"Then wouldn't this be the perfect time to rescue her?" I asked. "We can break in while they're partying. If she's in a silver cage in their basement, and they're all here, she's probably unguarded."

"We don't have the key," Efrain said. "Unless she's a shifter and can turn into a bird and fly out between the bars, the best bet now is to wait until they bring her to the clearing and then attack."

"The four of us against a whole pack?" I asked, mulling it over. "Okay, sounds like decent odds."

Oral grinned and squeezed my hand. "If those sound like good odds to you, I'm sticking right by your side."

"That's a good way to impress a lady," Nelson muttered. "Hide behind her."

"I'm a great shield," I said. "You should all hide behind me. No one will get hurt that way."

"Where's the fun in that?" Efrain asked. "This is an ambush. There's no fun without a fight."

"I'm going to scout for a lookout," Nelson said.

"I'm going, too," I said.

"Someone has to stay here," Efrain said.

"Then I'll stay," Nelson said. "You go."

"I'm going with Cayenne," Oral said.

"Pussy," Efrain muttered.

Oral just grinned, his ears poking out adorably. "They say you are what you eat."

"I'm going to look at the lodge," I said. "See if I can find any sign of her. If a couple of them are bringing her, then we'll only have to protect her from a few wolves instead of the pack. I'll put a shield around her, so they can't hurt her."

Efrain frowned, but at last he nodded. "Okay. Oral, if anything happens, squeal like a stuck pig."

"Got it," Oral said, snapping his fingers. "I'd say I could do a coyote song, but with my shifting abilities…"

He did not seem at all embarrassed by this admission. I'd have died of embarrassment if people teased me about my lack of magic. Not that they could, but if I'd been weak, I wouldn't have gone around talking about it.

With a promise to meet up in an hour, we split up. In the clearing below, a band had assembled on stage and struck up a jam. Kids my age were dancing in front of the stage in brightly colored dresses. The good-looking future king was dancing with a tall black girl. A white girl in a powder blue princess dress jumped around with an Asian girl in a royal blue mini dress. A pang of homesickness struck me. I should be with my own family right now, dancing around a fire and ushering in the eclipse that was just beginning to nibble at the edge of the moon.

Instead, I was alone in the woods with a man I hardly knew, though I couldn't deny I wanted to know more. It would be incredibly hard to leave him and his brothers when I had gotten Granny back. I had to prepare myself for that. For thanking them and walking away, back to my neat little life with my peaceful little coven and my sweet little intended. For never seeing Oral's goofy grin and Nelson's blazing eyes and Efrain's infuriating, irresistible smirk. I knew that no matter what happened, I'd always remember this day and the night before.

Always long for more.

How was it possible to miss home and, at the same time, want so badly for more than it offered?

"Penny for your thoughts," Oral said.

"I was just thinking," I said slowly. "That I'm going to miss you guys."

"Aww, hell, it doesn't have to be goodbye," he said. "You can have me in your collective any day you want, not just today." He gave me a wink, and my face warmed at the memory of how much I'd enjoyed having him for a day.

"I couldn't do that," I said. "I'd feel like I was using you."

"I'm here for the using," he said, holding aside a branch so I could go by without being scratched. I had to hand it to these rough boys, they sure knew how to make a lady feel special in a way that warlocks didn't bother with. Not that I needed a man to hold aside a branch, or open a door, or catch me when I tripped. It was the fact that they knew that but did those things anyway that made me feel special and cared for.

"Witches put a lot of thought into their collectives," I said. "We might have more than one relationship, but there's nothing casual about it. It's very deep and meaningful. We respect each member of our collective and take into account their feelings about other members."

"Sounds exhausting," Oral said with an easy grin. We skirted around a small log cabin and kept going toward the lodge on top off the hill.

"Okay, from what I've seen, it can be tiring," I admitted. "But if you choose wisely, it doesn't have to be."

"Well, I get along great with my brothers," Oral said. "So we'd be the perfect collective, I'd say."

"Really? Because it seems like Efrain might have trouble sharing."

"Nah," Oral said. "He's the middle child, so he acts out for attention. Trust me, we're all used to sharing. I just usually get the leftovers."

"As long as everyone is comfortable with their place."

"With you, maybe it would be different," Oral said. "Since you're not from our valley, and you don't see me that way. Although I guess now I've told you, so maybe you do." He scratched the back of his neck, ducking his head and grinning at me.

"You don't want to be in a witch's collective," I said. "You don't even like witches."

"I like one," he said. "And if we're going to go there, your people don't think much of shifters."

We passed another cabin, also empty, and kept climbing.

"Okay, that's true," I said. "But maybe it's time we do away with those prejudices."

"You sound like Dr. Golden."

I pulled up short, a little out of breath. "You know my aunt?"

Oral laughed. "Everyone knows Willow Golden. She's the only doctor in the shifter valley."

"Right," I said. "Of course."

I didn't know why I was surprised that he knew my aunt, the only witch-shifter around. Our worlds seemed so far apart, but now I was reminded that we lived just over a mountain from each other. It wasn't so far after all.

"Wait," I said. "If you know my aunt, does that mean… Is Efrain's Violet my cousin?"

"If Dr. G is your aunt, then that would be a yes."

I wanted to mull that over, but I had more important things to worry about. We came into view of the lodge just then, after passing several more log cabins. It was dark inside, with no lights in the windows.

Suddenly, my heart thudded hard in my chest. What if she wasn't there? What if they'd already…*sacrificed*…her? I'd never hold her hands again, their fingertips and palms thickly calloused from working, their backs soft and wrinkled as a tissue paper. I'd never see her beaming smile that made her eyes squeeze all the way closed, never hear her halting, wavery voice recount an adventure on the high seas or the heartbreak of an earth-shattering betrayal. My eyes burned, and my knees threatened to buckle with the weight of my grief.

As if sensing my distress, Oral's hand closed around mine. He gave me a sideways smile. "We'll find your granny," he said. "She'll be just fine."

"Thank you," I said, drawing a steadying breath. "Let's go see."

Oral balked. "Now?"

"When else? We're here and I don't see any guards. Let's check it out."

"You want to break into the pack leader's house?"

"Where's that big brave boar I saw earlier?" I asked, squeezing his hand this time.

141

"I think we left both of those back at the clearing."

"I think not," I said. "But if you're too scared to go with me, you can stand guard."

"No way," he said. "I'm not letting you go in alone."

I rolled my eyes and gave him a grin. "Then what are we waiting for?"

We crept up on the house from the back. It was huge and silent, looming under the moon, which was being swallowed by the red shadow of the earth.

"What's the plan here, Little Red?" Oral whispered.

"Let's try the door," I said. Witches pretty much never locked their doors, if they even had locks. From the little community gathering I'd witnessed earlier, I didn't think wolves would have much more security than we did.

I crept up the back steps quietly, though the house had a deserted air to it. It would have been nice to have my dad's mage magic, because in this case, I needed more than elemental magic to find my granny.

Robin squirmed in my hood, which I pulled up to quiet him further. He slept at night, but I was keeping him up with all the activity. "Get ready to help me out, little guy," I whispered.

Oral reached in front of me and turned the knob, pushing the door inwards and flattening us both against the wall beside it. Nothing happened.

"I'm going in," I said.

"You can't."

"Did you think I was just going to open the door and walk away?"

I pushed past Oral and stepped into the house. A board creaked under my foot and I winced, waiting for a wolf to leap out and gobble me up. But nothing happened.

"Let me shift," Oral said. "I can smell anything."

"As a pig?"

"We have excellent scenting ability."

"Really? I'd think as an animal that literally wallows in its own filth, that would be more of a hindrance than an advantage."

"Do you want to know if we're alone or not?"

"Yes, please," I said.

Oral peeled off his clothes with practiced speed. Seconds later, a boar was trotting around the huge lodge. After circling the large, open floorplan once, he shifted back into a man in front of me. I wondered how long it would take me to stop dropping my eyes to check out their bodies when they shifted.

Oral grinned. "No one here. Ninety percent chance there's no one upstairs. But there's a basement. We can check that."

"You got all that from one go-around?"

He scratched the back of his neck and grinned. "Not too shabby for an animal that wallows in its own filth, huh?"

"Sorry I said that," I said. "Let's check the basement."

Oral grabbed his clothes and headed for a door on the side of the kitchen, which turned out to be a pantry. The next one opened into a gaping blackness. "You don't happen to have a flashlight hidden anywhere in that ridiculous skirt, do you?"

"Better," I said, opening my palm and summoning a flame. Its flickering light barely illuminated the top steps of the ladder in front of us.

"This is it," Oral said, his Adam's apple bobbing as he swallowed.

"Yep."

"I wanted to say something," he said, grabbing my hand again.

"No goodbyes," I said. "We're going to get Granny. That's it."

I held the light aloft while Oral crept down the ladder. I crept along with him, facing forwards instead of facing the ladder, so I could watch his back. We descended into a dank basement, where I held up my flame. It was just a basement. My heart sank.

"She's not here," I said.

"Let me make sure," he said, dropping into a crouch and letting his boar out. He trotted to a short door in one dirt wall. I opened it and followed him through a short tunnel into another room, this one with a table and books. No silver cage. No torture chamber. No old woman.

We stepped through an open doorway into a basement bedroom. It even had a window. I cursed, disgusted. We'd wasted all this time coming here, only to find the house empty. I was about to turn back when my eyes fell on a door in the side of the bedroom. In a normal bedroom, it would house the closet. My heart hammered in my chest as I grabbed the doorknob. I squeezed my eyes closed, praying we'd find her just on the other side.

I pictured her stricken face, pinched with fear at first but quickly transforming to hope and joy when she saw me.

Turning the knob, I pushed open the door.

A set of stairs led up to another door. I tore through it, racing up the stairs, desperation stealing all reason. Bursting from the door at the top, I found myself outside the house.

No Granny.

The moon was half covered now. She wasn't here. They'd already taken her. I fell against the side of the house, a sob catching in my throat. "She's not here," I said, my voice blank despite the roiling emotions inside me.

"We'll find her," Oral said quietly.

I raised my eyes to his, letting myself voice my deepest fear for the first time. "What if we don't?"

"We will." He took my shoulders in both hands and looked me square in the eye. "I swear to you, Cayenne Golden, we will find your granny."

"You can't promise that."

"I don't care," he said. "I promise, anyway."

I wanted to scream in frustration, but that was probably not a good idea. I bit it back, letting Oral pull me into his arms instead. It boiled up in me, coming out as a growl. The next thing I knew, it had turned into a strangled sob. I collapsed against his chest, letting the grief wash over me. Big, ugly, hiccupping sobs wracked my body.

I'd come all this way, done all this, and Granny was still missing. I'd tainted my magic, had seen three men I admired rip apart someone with their teeth. And it had all been for nothing. Granny Golden was not here.

Chapter Eighteen

Cayenne

Oral kissed the top of my head, my forehead that had gone clammy from the damp night and the force of my anguish. When the sobs had died down, he cupped my face in his hands and lifted my mouth to his. His kiss held more than it had earlier, more tenderness, more depth. My heart swelled with enough warmth to choke off my breath, and my hands curled into his thick hair. My body pressed into his, wanting him closer still, wanting to let his concern swallow me and make me believe it could all be okay.

As much as I wanted to stay and explore this new feeling between us, both inside me and apparent in his kiss, that wouldn't get my granny back. I pulled away with a regretful pang.

"Aww, you're killing me, Little Red," he said.

"Great. Is that catching on?"

"Afraid so," he said with a grin. "Now, are you ready to go kick ass and take names?"

Over his shoulder, I caught sight of the swollen veil bleeding across the face of the moon. I should be with my parents, my sisters, my granny. My intended. Back in our own happy little coven. By now, my mom would be completely freaking out, and even calm Malik would be worried sick. The coven's entire ceremony was probably in disarray, upset by the disappearance of both me and Granny.

It was a miracle they hadn't already found me. If Mom had shown up at Nelson's house, she wouldn't have just gone home when he sent her away. She would have kept looking. And if she'd firebombed their house, how had they gotten away? It suddenly struck me that I didn't really know these guys at all. And what I knew…well, let's just say they had been good to me, but they hadn't exactly come across as men of high morals.

"When my mom blasted your house with fire," I said, my stomach suddenly twisting in a terrible way. "How did you and Nelson get away?"

"He had a protection charm on it," Oral said.

My eyes narrowed. "Where did he get that?"

"I don't know," he said. "Granddad left it with the house. A witch gave it to him at some point."

"What witch?"

"I don't know," Oral said, throwing up his hands. "It was back in grandpa's day. All I know is that Nelson brought it with us, even though it left his house vulnerable if anyone comes back."

"Why would he do that?"

"To protect you," Oral said, as if that were obvious.

"He barely knows me. Why would he risk his house for me?"

"Because you bewitched all of us," he said simply. "Whether you gave us healing magic or not."

"I didn't do anything," I said.

"You don't know what it's like in our valley," he said. "We've never been decent guys, and everyone knows it. And me—I'm the ugly stepchild of the bunch."

"You're not ugly," I said, my heart aching at the bitter edge that had crept into his easy manner.

"Be real, Cayenne," he said. "You've seen my brothers. I get the girls they won't take, and the girls they've broken who think it's payback to sleep with their brother. I'm the consolation prize at best, a tool for exacting revenge at worst. I don't get girls who want *me*. You made me think…maybe someday I could." He ducked his head and scratched the back of his neck again.

I remembered holding onto those ears, steering him with them. I remembered how good he'd made me feel today and how safe last night. "You could," I said fiercely. "You have."

He lifted his head and shrugged. "We'd better get back to the others. The sooner we get the protection back on Nelson's house, the better."

My heart squeezed at the thought of Nelson's house being destroyed while he was gone. Destroyed by my mother, because of me. Because I'd run off and wanted to save the day all by myself. And Nelson didn't need to do that—I had enough magic to protect myself. Despite the fact that I'd told him that, he'd been willing to risk all he had to make sure I lived. Suddenly, I thought I'd cry again. But I couldn't sit around bawling because I'd been stupid and reckless. The only way to fix this was to make sure I got back to my parents before they did something awful.

I grabbed Oral's hand, my fingers tight around his. "Let's go," I said, my voice hard with anger. "The bastard that took my granny is going to pay for this."

I marched off towards the clearing, not bothering to circle through the woods. A path led straight from the leader's lodge towards the clearing, and I was taking it. No more pussy-footing around. I was taking the direct route.

Chapter Nineteen

Efrain

While the little witch and Oral were off on their fruitless search, we raced back to our valley to check up on the invasion plans. King Owen, who was spending a little time in shifter jail, had broken out. I knew Cayenne didn't have the seeing stone. King Owen had it. For a minute, I wanted to rip apart the house in frustration. My plans could not implode. I'd come too far, fallen too far, to lose it all now.

"Our plans don't hinge on him," Zephyr said. As the heir to the shifter throne, he had a lot to say in the matter. He was right. Owen was a worthless bastard who had no business being our leader anyway—if you could call him that.

"I'll find him," I growled. The bastard wouldn't skip out on me when I came to get what I'd been promised.

"Good luck," Zephyr said. "He's probably headed for the border. The coward." He spit in the dirt behind the house, where he'd kept Owen in a shed.

"Did he leave anything?" I asked.

"He left the old witch's body," Zephyr said. "It's alive, but she's in some kind of trance. Knox saw a mouse come out of her pocket when she passed out, and the dumbass went after that and let Owen escape."

"What's a mouse got to do with anything?"

"It's where the witches store their souls," he said. "But it don't matter. The invasion will go ahead as planned."

I left the politics to the big brains. I was just a foot soldier. One with a job of his own to do before I joined in the battle to get some good hunting territory for the shifters.

"Here, take the witch with you," Zephyr said. "She might be a good bargaining tool if you find King Owen. I reckon he owes her big time now that she broke him out and he didn't stop to save her in return. And even a king knows not to fuck with witches."

A king, maybe, but my dumb ass couldn't seem to stop.

When he handed me a burnt-out lantern, I shrank back. Like Nelson's house, it had a magic block on it. The tiny cage was used to punish shifters after forcing them into the form of a small animal. They'd be locked in the lantern, unable to shift. And most small animals did not have long lifespans. I'd seen someone go into the lantern as a teenager and come out as a middle-aged man. Nature was largely indifferent to what form we took, but the laws of nature always applied. If you spent three months as a mouse, you'd come back to human form ten years older.

I took the lantern with the mouse inside, though. I didn't care if I caught Owen, but if I had the witch, she could witness me doing her bidding. She couldn't claim I still owed her.

Zephyr sent us back, assuring us the shifters were already assembling and on their way to the ambush. Nelson and I hurried to return to our meeting spot with Oral and Cayenne, still not speaking.

Finally, Nelson broke the silence. "I'm not going to hide what you're doing from Cayenne. It's wrong, Efrain."

"So is letting a witch curse your brother," I said. "If you can't watch, then go take up your position like Zephyr told us to."

Just then, Oral and Cayenne came marching through the woods.

"Show time," I said, my voice hard as flint. "Let's get this party started."

"Did you find Granny?" Cayenne asked. It was time she learned to stop trusting strangers, especially shifty shifters. Her mom obviously hadn't taught her the lessons she should have learned in life, so she was learning the hard way. But it was no longer my problem.

I heard the footsteps of other shifters in the woods all around us, creeping down the mountain.

"You need to go," I said to my brothers. "Get the hell out of here. This doesn't concern you."

I lifted my hands over Cayenne's head, letting the stone from Nelson's house fall into her cleavage. I'd tied it up with some string from the end of a bag of feed corn I'd found in the hunting lodge. Crushing down any remorse at snuffing her magic with such a cheap trick, I thought of Violet. But this time, even her image couldn't lighten the darkness of what I was about to do.

"No." Cayenne gasped and reached up, but I grabbed her hands and wrenched them behind her back.

"We all have our roles to play," I said. "It's not personal."

"What are you talking about?" she asked, beginning to struggle. "My magic! What did you do to my magic?" I forced my hands to stay closed around her slender wrists, forced my mind to feel nothing more for her than I'd felt for all the other women I'd fucked over.

"Go," I snarled at my brothers. "If you don't want to be in this position, don't cross a witch. Get out of here before she curses you, too."

"Let me go," Cayenne cried, stomping on my feet with her witchy boots. "I didn't curse you, but I sure as hell will if you don't release me."

I clenched my teeth and let the pain fuel my resolve. It didn't matter. She could curse me just like her grandma. It would never end. I'd grow old walking in place, never getting any closer, always one step behind that goddamn seeing stone. Violet had probably already forgotten me. It had been years.

"Efrain, we can't," Oral said, stepping forward.

"There's the witch right there in that cage," I said. "You think she'll have mercy on me, on any of us, if we release her? She's the one making me do this. Now get the fuck out before you're forced to do something worse to Cayenne."

Oral fell back, his eyes uncertain. He turned to Nelson, like he no longer trusted me. I didn't trust myself. I'd lost my goddamn mind. The last thread of my sanity was pulling awful tight. I could tell by the way I was wavering from finding Violet for the first time in years, the way I was tempted to pull Cayenne's struggling little body against mine, crush her to the ground and let her erase Violet from my memory once and for all.

They turned to go. Nelson's back was stiff, his shoulders taut. Oral's shoulders slumped as he trudged after my older brother.

"Nelson?" Cayenne asked, her voice higher than usual. She turned her pleading eyes on my brothers. "Oral? You can't do this. Don't believe him. I didn't curse you. I only have elemental magic."

"I know," Nelson said quietly. But he only paused a moment, then shifted into a boar and took off down the hill. When both my brothers were gone, I grabbed up the backpack and dragged out the red satin dress I'd brought for this occasion. It had belonged to Violet. She called it her seduction dress. It had worked on me. Now it was time for it to do its work on the alpha wolf.

"That's not my granny," Cayenne snarled. "My granny's not a shifter. Let me go right now, or I'll put a curse on you myself."

"You don't want to do that," I said. "That's your granny in that lantern, all right. She's not a shifter, but she somehow put her spirit in that mouse. If you want to bring it back to her body, you'll see it go right back into her. But first, you've got to do what she says. Just like I do."

I thrust the dress at Cayenne. "What are you doing?" she said, sounding horrified.

"I'm not doing anything," I said. "I've done my part. Now it's time for you to do yours. Are you going to put that on like your granny wants, or am I going to have to do it for you?"

Breathing hard from her struggle, she threw her hair back into my face. "I can't get dressed with my hands behind my back."

"Fine," I said. "Your granny is the one who put me in this position. This is what she wanted for me and for you. Do as she wants, and you'll never see me again."

"You'd better hope I don't," Cayenne said hotly.

I released her hands, and she immediately snatched the necklace off her neck. Before she could throw it, I grabbed her hand, closing my fingers around hers. Her free hand drew back and whipped across my cheek, stinging my skin like a hundred hornets.

I caught that hand, too, dragging both her hands behind her back again. Rage boiled in my chest, and I let it crush the growing voices inside protesting at what I was doing. "That wasn't very smart," I said. "If you think this is a joke, you're wrong. Your fate is sealed. Now let me have mine."

I ripped down the top of her ugly old dress, peeling it down her slim body. Her skin was warm against my hands, her limbs slender and fragile. I crushed my remorse. I felt nothing.

"Don't," she whispered.

"It's not me you should worry about," I said. "I promised I wouldn't touch you today, and the day's not over. You're not meant for the likes of me, Cayenne. You get a king. That's what your granny wanted for you. Royalty."

"Listen to me," she said. "You have it all wrong. My granny doesn't want me to do anything but be happy. She doesn't have a destiny planned for me. There's no reason for this. Witches don't believe in all this. We don't even have a queen."

"You'll have to ask her about that," I said, wrapping a vine around Cayenne's hands and pulling it tight. "I'm not royalty. I'm no one. A thug. A henchman. A good-for-nothing shifty shifter who follows orders. That's all I've ever been and all I'll ever be."

"That's not who you are. You're loyal, and passionate, and you tattooed a flower on your butt cheek for your girlfriend. You don't care what anyone thinks. And you're brave."

"I'm not brave," I snarled. "I'm a fucking coward like Oral. Those wolves I went after last night? That was me and my brothers, Cayenne. There were no wolves. Don't you get it? We set you up. We set it all up. We're not good people. Stop being naïve. It's not cute anymore."

I pushed her back into the leaves gently, although my anger was pulsing in my temples with every heartbeat.

"Please," she whispered as I ripped off the rest of her stupid dress.

"How many times do I have to tell you, I'm not after your body," I said. "I may be an asshole, but I'm not a rapist." I caught her feet and dragged the satiny dress over them, up over her trembling knees, her yielding thighs, her soft belly.

"Efrain, you're better than this," she whispered, trying to catch my gaze. I could feel the insistent pull of her eyes as she tried to ensnare me.

"No," I said, pulling her dress up over her creamy white breasts. "I'm not."

Chapter Twenty

Cayenne

My wrists were bruised and scraped as I tugged at the knotted vines, trying to break free. Robin could no longer feel my magic, and though he should have been sleeping, he was chirping in alarmed confusion instead. Efrain had taken pity on me when I started bawling at the thought of leaving my familiar, and he'd gently placed the bird on my shoulder, though it pecked at him and beat him with its wings. Now, I stumbled forward through the woods, Efrain guiding me as the moon slipped into the last sliver of the earth's shadow.

How could he do this to me? Tears stung my eyes as he marched me toward a fate I didn't understand. How could I have been such a fool? I'd wanted an adventure, and I'd done what I had to get it. I'd trusted these men, and they'd turned their backs on me. Not only turned their backs, but set me up. They'd lied the whole time. They'd only flirted with me to gain my trust, to flatter me, to toy with me. All along, they'd been planning this betrayal. The pain of it took my breath, sharp and raw across my newly blossoming heart.

"Listen to me," I begged, but Efrain was deaf to my pleas, as hard and unfeeling as a mountain. Efrain thought Granny had cursed him, and he was taking it out on me.

Where was she? I could almost bear all this if I knew it would save her. But she was not that mouse. There was only one person in our valley who could do that, and it wasn't my granny. It was Yvonne, the busy-body, nosy, youth-obsessed witch.

"Please, that's not my granny," I said desperately. "But I might know who it is."

"I don't give a damn who it is," Efrain said. "I owe her, and I'm paying my debt."

Worst of all, I could do nothing. I was helpless—pathetically devoid of power. I wanted to scream in frustration, to rip the necklace from my throat like a hot coal. I could feel its strong, blanketing magic all over my body, smothering my pores, my breath, my life. My own magic was writhing, panicking in claustrophobia. But it could do nothing, trapped under the weight of the cursed stone, as blocked as the huge moon above was blocked from the sun's path.

It hung huge above us, shadowed with red like an evil eye watching over the grim proceedings. Terror clawed up my throat as Efrain pushed me towards the clearing in this red dress, as if I were dressed for a sacrifice. Was this his plan to get into the pack? Was I the blood sacrifice?

Suddenly, the fire was blazing in front of us, just a few steps across the grass. People were undressing around the fire, and a girl with white hair was struggling in the pack leader's arms. Was this an exchange? Me for the white-haired girl?

Efrain pushed me roughly into the clearing, and I stumbled, my feet catching in the dress. I fell, unable to stop myself with my hands bound.

"Efrain, no," I said. And then, with the clarity of a seeing stone, I saw the futility of my protests. As he spoke above me, my purpose crystallized. He wanted me to marry this man I'd never met in my life. I should have found it ironic. I'd fallen for Efrain and his brothers in a day, and yet, the shock of being told I was to be claimed by this handsome stranger made my head swim. Their words lost meaning as they negotiated my marriage above my head, without my consent.

Hysterical, furious words slammed through my head like waves. I wanted to scratch Efrain's eyes out, to blast fire out of every magic outlet in my body, to smash him under a giant boulder and leave him as struggling and helpless as I was. But I had no magic, no power whatsoever.

Efrain was telling them I was a shifter, and I realized then my mistake. I'd naively assumed that because I cared about them, they cared about me. But they hadn't cared. I was just a pawn in their game, their turf war with the wolves. Not only did they not care about me, they didn't even know who I was. They thought I was someone else, a shifter, the granddaughter of a mouse.

I could no more bring about a marriage alliance between their warring tribes than a regular human could. Wolves and witches were incompatible. Wolves mated with one person for life and obeyed one patriarchal ruler. Witch society was the opposite of theirs in every way.

I focused instead on something I could control—my hands. Working my raw wrists against the vines, I began to loosen them while Efrain was busy with the alpha wolf. The world around me seemed to slow, expand, and then shrink. And then it snapped. Everything happened at once.

Efrain dropped the lantern with the mouse shifter. The white-haired girl dove for it as Efrain shifted and the alpha wolf attacked. My wrist came free.

Without bothering to free my other hand, I ripped away the stone. The moment it was off my body, I erected a shield around myself. Robin plunged through and dove into my hair, rubbing his feathery body against my head, and relief washed over me. I was safe. I had my magic and my familiar.

Around me, wolves dove at shifters who were emerging from the woods. A boar ran past me, and a cry caught in my throat. It was none of my business what happened to them. They had used me, and when their plan failed, they had no more use for me. And I had no use for them.

I sat in the clearing, watching the chaos as if it were a movie. I watched a bear rip a wolf's head from its body. Another boar—Oral—ran to me, but I wouldn't let him in. My shield was an impenetrable fortress, just like my heart. I would never let them in again. They could go be eaten by wolves for all I cared. They'd literally thrown me to the wolves, and I wanted nothing to do with them.

I met Oral's little piggy eyes, and I didn't feel a thing. Not even when I saw the pleading in them. He pushed at my shield, and I pushed him back with the shimmering wall of magic. "Go away," I said. "You chose your side, and I'm not on it. Witches are Switzerland, Oral."

He pawed at the ground and tried to puncture my magic with his tusk. But my magic was smarter than my heart, and it refused to be breached by the kindness in his eyes.

"Good luck," I called as he turned away. "I hope you don't die."

The head, shoulder, and neck of a stag landed on my shield, smearing down the side of it. I screamed and scrambled back, my concentration broken. For a second, the walls around me slipped. I choked back a gasp, my last words to Oral scrolling through my mind like a prophecy. I didn't want him to die.

But I couldn't let myself care. I couldn't. He and his brothers were pigs who cared only about themselves. He hadn't stopped Efrain. When I'd needed him and Nelson, he'd turned his back on me. I was just giving them a taste of their own medicine.

A black and white wolf gave a spine-shattering howl and charged off into the woods. My eyes dropped back to the deer's head. That wasn't just a deer. It was a person. A human being. A man who might be loved or feared, who had experienced his own anxieties and adventures, bravery and betrayal.

My head snapped up. Granny. Where was she?

If she'd had magic, my own magic could have called out to hers and found her. But she wasn't here. I knew that now. I didn't know if she'd ever been here, but I didn't think so. Which meant she was still missing, out there somewhere waiting for me to find her. For the first time since Efrain had told me she was gone, I realized how big this was. I was nothing but a sheltered little girl like he'd said. Sure, my magic was strong, but I couldn't count on that alone to save me.

Once this battle was over and the blood had been shed, someone would realize what I was—that I wasn't a shifter at all. That I had magic that they could use and exploit in their battles, just like my mother had warned. Whichever side won, they would want me to join them. And if I wouldn't join by choice, they might do what Efrain had done and make me join by force.

Not. Gonna. Happen.

Rage swelled inside me, not the furious kind that tore like a windstorm inside, but the quiet, deadly kind. I raised my head, gathering my magic, and looked at the big red moon. Wolves were howling in the woods. Animals were whimpering around me. I was in a world so far from mine I could not comprehend the brutality. Not wanting to see more, I closed my eyes. Lifting my hands, I shot a blast of magic like a beacon into the sky.

Chapter Twenty-One

Cayenne

Within minutes, my mother and several of my fathers were standing outside my shield. Fox knelt at the edge and held out a hand to me. "Cayenne," he said firmly. "Let us come in."

"Dad," I whispered, choking on my relief when I saw the concern in his soft brown eyes.

"Drop the shield," he said.

"We're trespassing," Mom said. "We should hurry back."

Back to the First Valley. The thought had never seemed so sweet. My shield fell away like a wall of water crashing to the ground, and I dove to my feet, burying myself in my mother's arms. "You were right," I blubbered. "It's horrible out here. I'm so, so sorry, Mom."

She stroked my hair behind my ear, holding me while I clung to her. Two of my dads joined our circle, their arms wrapping around us protectively.

"Where did everyone go?" I asked at last, lifting my head. Bodies were spread over the clearing, some of them human and some animal. In the distance, I could hear the wolves howling. I didn't know if that meant they'd chased the shifters out, or the shifters had chased them out. It didn't matter.

"They must have taken the fight elsewhere," Quill said.

Fox cracked his knuckles. "It's been too long since I had a proper fight."

"No," Mom said. "Let's go home. Cayenne needs to recover."

I tried not to look at the corpses, but I couldn't stop my eyes from searching. At the far side, I spotted a boar, its bristles gleaming faintly in the firelight. I couldn't tell who it was, but my stomach heaved. I bit back a scream, lurching in that direction.

"Cayenne," Quill said, stopping me with his firm tone. "This isn't our fight. You should never have been here at all."

"He's right," Mom said, her tone gentler. "You can't help them now. They're gone. There's nothing you could have done."

"No," I whispered. It couldn't be true. It couldn't.

I could have let Oral into my shield. If it was him, I was to blame for his death. And even if it was Efrain or Nelson,

I could have protected us all. I could have put them all in my shield.

Another howl sounded, this one closer and full of anguish. Wolves had died, too. One lay bleeding not far from me, whimpers escaping its muzzle with every breath.

"We need to go," Mom said. "It's not safe here. There are too many wolves and not enough of us."

I knew she was right. I remembered Efrain's words when he'd lured me out of my grandma's cottage. *Sometimes the bravest thing you can do is run.* And even though he'd turned out to be a lying bastard, he'd made himself believable by mixing in words of truth.

It was time to run. Time to get help. Time to stop believing I could defeat anything. In the end, I'd been defeated by something worse than an enemy. I'd been defeated by myself—my pride, my stubbornness, and my stupid, vulnerable, blind heart.

My parents had to support me, half dragging me away, leaving my heart behind. I'd lost it to three pig-men, and I didn't know if I'd ever get it back. My legs refused to move, to carry me further and further from my heart with every step.

"You want to tell us what you were doing here?" Fox asked cautiously when we reached the top of the mountain that formed the border between our valley and that of the wolves.

"I thought they had Granny Golden," I said, closing my eyes for a second. The ache behind them had not subsided since leaving the clearing.

I could have saved him. Maybe I couldn't have saved Granny, but I could have saved the pigs.

"Why did you think that?" Mom asked.

"She wasn't home," I said. "And one of the shifters told me the wolves had her."

"You don't have to explain," Quill said, patting my back like I was a little girl again. "Not tonight, anyway."

"We have to find her," I said, pulling away. "She's in danger. I'm sure of it. It looked like she'd been gone for a while."

Quill frowned. "I was going to the cottage this evening to get you both, but one of the other witches said she was going that way and she'd deliver a message."

"Who?" I asked, but I already knew the answer.

"Yvonne," Mom said, her brows furrowing.

"We'll look into it," Quill said. "You just worry about getting some rest and cleansing your magic."

"But I have to find her."

"No," he said. "You don't. You need to go home. And that's an order from your father, young lady."

And even though I wanted to find Granny so bad it hurt, to tell her everything and have her weathered old hands stroke back my hair, have her tell me in her faltering way that it would all be okay and that she'd seen worse—even though

I would have given anything to find her, for once I was glad to have a small army of parents to order me around.

Chapter Twenty-Two

Nelson

I woke up in a fog. A lady with two long blonde braids bent over me.

"You're awake," she said. "That's good. Your brothers were afraid they'd lost you for good."

"They're okay?"

"They're fine," she said, sitting down carefully on the edge of my bed. "How are you feeling?"

"Like I've been drugged," I said, trying to push myself up to sitting. But something wasn't working right. My whole body was stunned with pain, but it was a dull ache that I only vaguely felt. More than that, I felt myself tipping sideways.

Dr. Golden straightened me and offered a sad smile. "Painkillers."

"Where's Cayenne?"

"My niece?" she asked, drawing back. Obviously she had no idea why I was asking.

"Did the wolves get her? The pack leader? Did he marry her?"

Dr. G looked at me like maybe I'd hit my head in the battle. "Cayenne's at home, and she's fine. As for the pack leader, he's not going to be marrying anyone anytime soon," she said. "He was severely injured, like a lot of wolves and a lot of shifters. That includes you, Nelson."

Maybe I did hit my head…

I was so tired I had to close my eyes again. At least Cayenne had escaped. Efrain's stupid plan had failed. I didn't know if that meant that he was still cursed and in debt to the witch, or if he'd fulfilled his end of the bargain by throwing her to the wolves. I didn't the energy to think about it. It was enough to know she was okay.

*

Oral

I didn't want to be in the room when Dr. Golden told him, but Efrain said he'd kick my ass right up to my throat if I wussed out. I wasn't good at that kind of shit. I was good at making pancakes and cheering girls up, at making off-color jokes that got my boneheaded brothers to laugh and ease up when they were fighting.

"My arm?" Nelson asked, staring blankly at Dr. Golden. He moved his shoulder, his eyes falling on the blankets where his limb ended. Then he stopped moving without uncovering it.

"Your right side is completely uninjured," she said gently. "And it's possible your left leg will make a full recovery. You can still lead a full life. Not everyone who was there that night is so fortunate."

"And they make prosthetics now," I offered. "You can get a bionic hand. You'll be like a cyborg, bro."

He glared at me, his face a mixture of bewilderment and fury.

"It could be worse," I said, shoving my hands in my pockets, like I could hide the fact that I still had two.

"How?" he asked.

"You could have lost your dick," Efrain offered.

"I might as well have," Nelson said. "Name one woman who would take a man with a gimp leg and a stump."

"Well, you don't gotta marry her," Efrain said. "If she's just here for the night, she don't care what your arm and leg are going to do for her."

Nelson's head dropped back on the pillow, and his eyes fell shut. In that moment, I would have given him one of my hands if it could bring his back. Nelson wanted something Efrain and I didn't—at least, not yet. He wanted a good wife to provide for and a little family to put in his big, strong house. Up until a few days ago, we'd thought he was headed that way, settling down, quitting the wild lifestyle we carried on. When I'd seen him looking at Cayenne the way he had, I'd known the end was near. I just didn't know it would end like this.

While Dr. Golden went over the long-term plan with Nelson, I pulled Efrain out into the hall.

"Maybe we should get Cayenne," I said, speaking her name for the first time since that night.

Efrain snorted. "She's never coming back here."

"She has healing abilities."

"So does Dr. G," he said. "She's a witch, too, remember?"

I gave him a look.

He played dumb.

"There's more to her healing abilities than magic," I said. "And you know he could use a girl who didn't make him feel like a cripple. Besides, Cayenne doesn't need anyone to take care of her, so he wouldn't feel bad that he couldn't provide. She'll have a whole mess of husbands around."

"So now you're throwing him to the witches to make a marriage alliance? I thought that was their job."

"And yours," I shot back.

"I did it for them."

"That's almost as sorry an excuse as saying you did it for Cayenne so she could be a queen," I said. "You did it for Violet, and you know it."

He glared at me, then slumped against the wall. "Fine, I did it for Violet."

I watched him for a minute to make sure he wasn't in an ass-kicking mood. "So how come you haven't gone after her? You repaid the witch."

"King Owen says he'll see about getting me the Eye of Odin."

Neither of us said anything for a minute. Dr. Golden's soft, weary voice went on in the room behind us. She hated all this fighting. She'd been trying to do her job peacefully despite the tensions between the valleys. I could hear the consternation in her voice even as she tried to be gentle.

Finally I asked a question just so I didn't have to hear her and know my brother was in there, a broken, diminished version of his old self. "Why?"

"Why's he getting me the stone? I don't know, maybe so I'll throw his daughter to the wolves and hope their alpha likes blondes more than he liked redheads."

"No, why are you so fixated on getting Violet back? She was a bitch, bro. And I don't think you even loved her half so much when she was here."

"But what kind of man dumps his high school sweetheart when she's abducted?"

"Men like us," I said. "Since when do you care what people think of you?"

He shrugged. "Maybe I don't want to be a 'man like us' all my life. One day, I'd like to be more than that asshole who cheated on some woman with her sister."

"You're already more than that."

175

Efrain crossed his arms and frowned at the floor. "One day, I'd like to be somebody's hero."

"There's a girl right over the mountain who wants to find her granny something awful."

"I can't go over there," he said. "She'll light me on fire."

"Coward."

"I don't see you offering to go into the witch valley to talk to her."

"I'm a coward, too. Plus, I didn't toss her to the wolves. You owe her. Go redeem yourself."

"And what are you going to do to redeem yourself?"

"I'm going to make you do the right thing," he said. "Someone's gotta stay here with Nelson, anyway. When you get back here with her, I'll have dinner waiting."

"I know you're trying to impress her, but I don't think Cayenne likes chicks."

"One, she seemed pretty impressed after I went down on her, and two, chicks dig a guy who cooks. I'm versatile. You've got exactly one thing going for you, and all you have to do is look at Nelson to see how quick that can be taken from you."

"Don't make me hurt you."

"Shut up and go get our girl."

*

Efrain

You'd think that witches would just put a spell on their valley so no one could enter uninvited. But maybe that took too much magic or something. I didn't really know a lot about witches, despite the fact that I'd hung around Violet for years. She said she didn't have magic, and since she was raised in the shifter valley, she didn't care for witches.

When I stepped over the border into their territory, no lightning bolt struck me down. My legs did not turn to stone, an impenetrable fog did not swallow me whole, and I didn't find myself walking backwards across the boundary again. The only thing that happened was that a pain twisted my insides. The last time I'd come here, I'd been following Cayenne back to her granny's house, thinking this would be over quickly.

I didn't know if it would ever be over now, but I welcomed the aching clench in my gut. It was the first time I'd felt anything in days—since the night I'd thrown her at the wolf king's feet and told him to have at her. What had I done?

My feet began to move quicker, drawing me down the mountain at a faster clip. The thought of seeing her again spurred me on. Even though she'd probably smash my head in with a rock again, it would be worth it to see her. This time,

I'd deserve it. Hell, I guess I'd deserved it the last time, too. I'd been using her, plotting against her, the whole time.

All for Violet, the damn psycho I'd been about to drop for good when she'd disappeared. I couldn't just say good riddance when my girlfriend disappeared without a trace. So I'd held on, making it something it never had been in reality. I'd made myself believe that I could be a hero, that I could save her, and that if I did, she'd love me again, the way she had when we were kids. Like Oral said, though, that had already been gone when she left. It had faded years before, leaving nothing between us but the bickering of two people who are more like siblings than lovers.

I stopped, my breath catching in my chest, burning through my lungs.

What had I done?

For years I'd searched. I'd built a fantasy in my head, built a girl in my head who had never existed. I'd used her as an excuse for every shitty thing I did, for running from responsibility, for treating other women like nothing, the way she'd treated me. They hadn't mattered. None of them had mattered. Only Violet had mattered.

And now that she didn't....

I punched the nearest tree trunk just to feel the pain, to draw some of it outside my chest. I did it again, letting the rough bark bite into my knuckles and rip open my skin. If my hand hurt like hell, I could focus on that, not the scraped-out hollow inside me.

I had to find Cayenne. I would find her, would tell her this. I'd tell her I wasn't looking for Violet anymore, that I'd given up.

Except giving up wasn't the right word for it. I'd seen the light.

What if it was too late? I'd fucked up so bad Cayenne might never forgive me, might never look at me with those trusting, flashing eyes. I had to find her, to get her back. Not just for me, but for my brothers, who needed her even more than I did.

When I heard voices ahead, I broke into a jog. Leaves crunched and twigs snapped under my feet as I ran, urgency growing inside me with every step. That might be her. I had to reach her.

The forest ended abruptly, spitting me out into a clearing. A small stone house stood to my right, the front lined with a row of picnic tables laden with food. The clearing was full of people standing with their backs to me. On a raised stone altar in front of them, two people stood facing each other across a ball of fire. One of them was a short black guy with an easy smile on his face. The other was a girl in a fancy white dress with a mass of pepper-red waves blowing in the wind behind her and a robin on her shoulder.

I didn't have to know a lot about witches to know what I was seeing. An anguished shout tore from my throat. "No!"

Without thinking, I charged through the crowd to rescue my little red witch.

Chapter Twenty-Three

Cayenne

My concentration, which had already been full of fissures, broke completely when I heard the deep, desperate cry rip from the crowd. My heart was born and died again in that moment, sure that I'd heard the impossible. The ball of magic between me and Malik fizzled and spit as it fell to the ground and spun out its energy.

"Cayenne, no," Efrain said, lurching through the front of the crowd and coming to a halt in front of us. My parents, who stood at the front of the coven, shifted and glanced at each other. But one of my dads gripped Mom's shoulder when she tried to step forward.

"What are you doing here?" I hissed, narrowing my eyes at the man who had tricked me, who had got me all turned around and twisted inside out and then used it to his advantage.

"I—I know where your grandma is," he said.

"I've heard that one before."

He seemed to notice our audience and his voice faltered. "At least…I'm pretty sure."

"Do you really think I'm stupid enough to fall for that again?"

"You're not stupid," he said. "I know where I went wrong. That wasn't your grandma at all."

"You think?" I asked through clenched teeth, fury boiling inside me. My hands clenched, holding back the sparks that threatened to burst into flames in my palms.

"Who's this?" Malik asked quietly.

"This is Efrain," I said. "The guy who tried to sell me down the river to the wolves."

Malik took a step forward, his own hands curling into fists. "So you're the reason Caye's been crying for days?"

I wanted to fire blast him for saying that, but Efrain's brow furrowed with confusion and…concern. "No," he said, his eyes searching my face. "Tell me that's not true."

"It's not," I said. "I'd never cry over a pig like you. Now why don't you go find your precious Violet and tattoo her face on your other butt cheek."

"I don't care about Violet," he said. "I made a mistake, Cayenne. Let me make it up to you."

My fury broke through the dam holding it back.

"Make it up to me?" I screamed, throwing a punch. "You lied to me from the moment we met, tricked me and led me into the middle of a slaughter, and offered me up as a sacrifice."

As I screamed the words at him, the pain swelled in me like I was reliving the awful moment, the moment I'd realized that I was nothing to him. My fists pummeled his back and shoulders, but he barely flinched. He covered his head with his hands but didn't step out of the way or try to stop me. He was a wall of muscle, unyielding under the flurry of blows. Rage washed over me, coloring my world red as blood, black as my magic. I jumped onto his back, raining blows on his head. I wanted to kill him, to destroy him like he'd destroyed me.

I couldn't even find joy in my wedding because of him. Because how could I trust anyone when I'd been so wrong about him? Because how could I be happy knowing that three quarters of my heart lived over a mountain, inside a bunch of pigs who had stolen it and gobbled it up as easily as apple droppings?

Before I had spent my fury, I felt myself being lifted, heard the ripping of fabric as Efrain shifted. He charged forward, skirting the crowd. I heard Malik call my name, but I was lost in my own fury. "Put me down," I yelled, slapping the stallion's side.

He only charged forward faster, racing through the woods. I grabbed at a branch, came away with only leaves. I threw them at his head, then ducked, flattening myself when he dove under a branch. He galloped up the mountain, climbing and sliding. I grabbed at another branch, coming away from this one with a scraped palm and a torn, thin branch. Slapping him with the makeshift switch, I bit down on my tongue, tasting the salt of my tears. I didn't know when I'd started crying.

It hadn't dispelled my anger, my hurt. I twisted one hand into Efrain's mane and swung the flexible branch, burning it into his flanks. "What are you going to do now, tie me up and force me on a man I've never met?" I asked, slapping him with the stick again and again. "Oh, wait, you already did that. How about steal me away from my own wedding? Right, you did that, too. You could always pretend to give a shit about me while all along planning to sell me into captivity for a couple acres of hunting ground. Is there anything you haven't done?"

Efrain stopped abruptly at the top of the mountain, and I nearly flew off his back into the clearing around the lighthouse, where we'd first met. My breath caught in my throat for a second, and then I slid off his back, breathing hard.

"Is this your attempt at reminding me of our sweet first encounter?" I asked, the switch still clutched in my hand. "Because it wasn't sweet, Efrain. You were a bastard from the moment we met, and you'll never be anything but a cold-hearted, greedy little pig." I could feel blood squeezing out of the cuts I'd gotten tearing the switch from the tree, but I only tightened my grip, relishing the sting.

He reached out, grabbing my white dress with his teeth and ripping it open down the front.

"Hey," I yelled, smacking his cheek with my bleeding palm.

His teeth yanked again, and the lace tore further, revealing my breasts. His eyes on me made my whole body seethe with desire, and I remembered the way he'd made me feel, the way they all had. That animal inside me woke to meet his.

I grabbed his head between my hands and pulled his muzzle up to my face. "Shift," I commanded.

He obeyed. For a second, we stood staring at each other, our breath coming fast and hard in the cold air. My pulse began to race wildly as I took in his form, fully human and fully ready, his body demanding mine. I leapt at him, knocking him backwards, not sure what I wanted more—to destroy him or devour him. He stumbled, and his arms wrapped around me, dragging me to the ground with him. I rolled over onto him, yanking at my torn dress, trying to free myself of the last thing that stood between us. Efrain grabbed it with both hands and shredded it as easily as he shredded his own clothes when he shifted, tossing into the grass beside us.

He took one look at me, flipped me onto my back, and with one powerful thrust, took my virginity. I cried out in shock and pain, and Efrain growled, biting down on my shoulder as he erased my innocence one sure stroke at a time. After a minute, the pleasure overtook the pain, and I dug my nails deep into his skin, shredding it like he'd shredded my dress. I pulled him closer, deeper, harder, until we couldn't bear another moment, and we were both lost to everything but each other. My magic pulsed out, shimmering around us for a second before swallowing him in one giant gulp.

Chapter Twenty-Four

Cayenne

"You made me bleed, you little devil," Efrain said, reaching around his thick body to swipe at a drop running down his back.

"Then consider us even," I said, pointing to a scarlet splotch in the smashed, papery grass where we'd lain, now bleached to the color of bones. "What do you think that is?"

"Oh, shit," Efrain said, his brows drawing together. "Sorry. I forgot about that."

"I'm fine," I said, rolling my eyes as I drew on my tattered dress. "Thanks for asking."

"Oh," Efrain said again. "Right. So…am I supposed to get you roses or something?"

I closed my eyes for a second before answering. "Do shifters have some special deflowering ritual that requires you to provide me with literal flowers in return for my virginity?"

He scowled. "No."

"Neither do witches," I said. "Though I would ordinarily ask you to join my collective at this point if not sooner."

"Wait, you're asking me to marry you?"

"Is that a problem?" I asked, tossing my tangled hair back.

"I… No," Efrain said, looking a bit bewildered by his own answer.

"Good," I said.

"It's not a problem for me," Efrain said. "I can't speak for your other husband."

"Malik wants me to be happy," I said. "He'll accept my choices. And so will the rest of the coven." It was true. They believed in free will. No one got married against their will in the Winslow Witch coven.

Efrain shook his head. "He's a bigger man than me, then."

"I don't think that's possible," I said, my eyes lingering on the menagerie of tattoos across his chest. I reached out and traced my fingertips along the serpent that climbed his ribs. A tremor went through his skin, and a chill swept over him at my touch. My own familiar stirred sleepily against my neck, content now that I'd claimed Efrain with my magic.

"Your brothers," I said, guilt suddenly flaring inside me. "They're both…Did they survive?"

"They're alive," he said. "They'll be fine with it. But are your parents really going to be okay with this?"

"They might not be very happy about it," I admitted. "We don't have to get married right away, though. You can be my intended as long as you want."

"We don't have to wait until then to fuck, right? Because I'm not really into the whole delayed gratification thing."

"Obviously," I said. "And no. I'm not trying make you a gentleman. But you do know I'll be with the others, too. Not just you. And you can't be with other women."

"Who are the others?"

Now it was my turn to hesitate. Somehow, I'd thought it was assumed that if I took him, I was taking them all. But I would have to ask them each individually, of course.

"Malik and your brothers," I said. "If you think they'll have me."

"You won't have to ask Oral twice," he said. "But Nelson…he might play hard to get. He was injured pretty bad in the fight."

I held my dress closed, as if it could keep my heart in my chest. "How bad?" I whispered.

"He lost one arm clear up to the elbow," Efrain said. "And his leg's pretty torn up, too, but Dr. Golden thinks he'll be able to walk again."

I sucked in a breath, not just because something so gruesome had happened. The way Efrain said it, as if it were commonplace, made me both sick and sad for them. They hadn't lived easy, peaceful lives like I had. I couldn't pity them for it, though. That was what had drawn me to them.

"Let's see about your granny," Efrain said, turning to the tower.

"You were serious?"

"Did you think I came to kidnap you from your wedding just so I could ravish you?"

"Well…"

He gave me a mean side-eye. "I'm not that bad."

I matched his look with one of my own.

"Damn, you're right. I'm that bad," he said. "But I know where I went wrong. This old lady witch came to me and told me her granddaughter lives in this tower. So when I saw you outside it, I thought you were her."

"What does that have to do with Granny Golden, though?"

"I think the witch lives here," he said.

"No one lives here. There's no door."

We studied the lighthouse. The doors had been sealed, with only the empty windows looking down on us from above. "I'll fly up and check," Efrain said.

"Wait," I said, striding to the willow tree. I picked up a broken limb and closed my eyes, feeding air magic into it.

"What are you doing?" Efrain said as I straddled the stick.

"I'm a witch," I said, tossing my hair back. "I find alternatives when I don't have a broomstick on hand."

189

TWISTED

Efrain stretched up on tiptoes, aiming his arms upwards like he was above to execute a dive into the sky. His muscles bunched and bulged, and I let myself openly admire him this time. Seconds later, his body seemed to explode into blackness, and a raven emerged from the spot where he'd been. I sucked in a breath even though I'd known it was coming. He circled me, showing off his sleek feathers and mastery of wings.

I ignored him and summoned more magic. Witches didn't really fly—not often. It took a lot of magic to lift an entire person. The wind around us began to swirl, and slowly, I lifted off the ground, buffeted by the air current I was creating. When we reached the window, Efrain swooped inside.

Irritation rose in me. I wished I could fly so easily, go check out the room before him. Instead, I had to grip the edge of the window and keep myself airborne at the same time. Before I could climb inside, Efrain appeared at the window in human form, grabbing both my hands and pulling me up and in. I crashed against his muscled body then pulled away, tossing my hair back and trying to catch my breath.

Efrain smirked. "You okay there, Little Red?"

"Fine," I said. "Don't gloat. And if you're planning to lock me in here—" I broke off when I saw the room behind him. Shoving him out of the way, I ran to the bed. "Granny," I cried, throwing myself onto her. Her body was limp under mine, heavy and unmoving. Tears ached behind my eyes as I sat up and looked at her ancient, wrinkled face that had known so much heartbreak—her husband's betrayal, then his evil, the extinguishing of her internal flame, which fueled a witch's magic.

"Granny?" I whispered, touching her cold cheek. "No…" I shook her, hard, but her body barely moved. Her eyelids were still, her lips slightly parted and pulled down at the corners by gravity. She didn't even look like my granny.

"Hey, it's gonna be okay," Efrain said, resting his huge hands on my shoulders. He gently drew me back and bent over her, pulling her arm from under the quilt. She was tucked into the bed, which was a wooden frame holding a soft, slightly lumpy mattress and covered with the most intricate quilt I'd ever seen. I hadn't even noticed it when I'd seen her face peeking out from under it. But now, as I waited for Efrain to find her pulse, my eyes fell on the scene. It was one giant scene instead of patchwork, depicting what looked like the summertime view of one of the valleys from above. Each tree was individually cut and sewn with the kind of tiny, even stitch that a machine would make—but there was no way it could stitch around each puffy green tree.

"She's got a pulse," Efrain said, sinking onto the edge of the bed. His relief was so evident it made tears blur over my eyes again. I scooted over, curling my body against his as we sat looking down at her.

"Why won't she wake up?" I asked.

"I don't know," he said. "Maybe we should go get Dr. G."

"I'm not leaving her."

"Okay, okay," he said, holding up both hands. "We'll wait for her to wake up."

I shifted, and as I did, something grated strangely under my boot. I looked down to see my foot resting on a pile of…human hair. "Ew," I cried, kicking it under the bed. Who would need a wig in a place like this?

"I'll wait," I said, an uneasy feeling rising in my belly. "I can't leave her alone. You go get Dr. G."

"I can't leave you alone," he said.

"I have my magic," I said, though I'd felt a little less confident since he'd bound it so easily. But that was my mistake. I'd trusted him, and he'd betrayed me. No one could overpower me here if they came back and found me with Granny. The only way to defeat me was to gain my trust, like Efrain had. And it would take a long time before I trusted a stranger again.

He frowned and glanced around the room. "I don't like it."

"If you want to prove to me that I can trust you, then bring the doctor," I said. "And don't worry about me. Half the coven is outside this tower."

"What?" His eyes popped wide and his nostrils flared.

I gave him a smug smile. "You don't think they'd just let you run off with me," I said. "They came after us. You'd better go explain yourself to them before they decide to shoot you with magical fireballs first and ask questions later."

"Would they do that?"

"Trust me, you don't want them to," I said. "It hurts a lot."

"Well, shit," Efrain said, standing and looking down at his naked body. "Are they going to see me and think I raped you? Your dress is all torn."

"I'll give them a wave while you fly down," I said.

"Can you tell them what happened, too, so they don't burn me into crispy bacon?"

"I'll leave you to do the explaining," I said. "It'll be your first test as my intended. You've got to win over my parents, you know. Oh, and my other fiancé. You'll need to be on good terms with him before you join my collective."

"So that's how this is going to be."

"Yep," I said. "Welcome to married life."

"Shit," he said, hooking a finger in the tear in my dress and tugging it aside. "Can't we just keep each other happy at night? And let one of the other husbands cook for you and all that shit?"

"That's how you did it before, right? You and Nelson got the ladies at night, and Oral got to cook for them?"

"He got them in the morning," Efrain said. "Trust me, he did more than cook for them."

"And how many of those women stuck around?" I asked.

"Fine," he said. "You signal them that I'm okay, and I'll go talk to them."

"Get the doctor first," I said. "Then you can talk to them."

193

I went to the window and waved to Malik and my parents, who all stood below the tower. A handful of other witches and warlocks stood in the clearing, waiting.

"We found Granny," I hollered down to them. "Efrain's going to fly to get Dr. Golden."

"Is she okay?" Quill called up.

"I don't know," I said.

"I'm coming up," he said.

"You better go," I said to Efrain. I stood on tiptoes to kiss him, a thrill of pleasure going through me at how small I felt with his huge hands around my waist and his thick arms around my body.

"You better stop kissing me," he said. "There's no hiding anything when I'm naked."

"Go on," I said, swatting his muscular backside. "Oh, and by the way, I'm going to need you to get that tattoo removed from your ass."

Chapter Twenty-Five

After Efrain shifted and flew out the window, I returned to the bed and took Granny's hand. A minute later, Quill scrambled through the window.

"How is she?" He looked around the room. "What is this place?"

I hadn't taken time to look around. Efrain had surveyed the room as a bird, but he'd just checked that it was safe. Now, as I studied my surroundings, prickles crawled up my spine. I was inside the lighthouse with no door. It wasn't the usual upstairs of a lighthouse, with a light, though. It had been made into a large room, and the light was gone. As I took in the clothes hanging on pegs along a section of wall, a counter with a small sink and a few dishes in a rack beside it, and a bookshelf with creased paperbacks, my stomach began to shake.

"Daddy," I whispered. "Efrain's right. Someone lives here."

"Yeah," he said, his voice quiet. Soberly, we surveyed the paintings on the walls—elaborate, detailed, if slightly repetitive scenes of the Ozark Mountains. If I was going to paint something up here, I'd paint where the lighthouse came from. There were so many things I wanted to see that I hadn't, places I wanted to go again, and things that drew my interest more than the valleys around me—the beach with its hot sand and strange smells, cities with their lights twinkling like stars close enough to reach out and touch, craggy mountains that jutted so far into the sky they had their own climate.

And people. Tribes that painted their faces with intricate patterns, women in brightly colored saris, street performers, musicians, acrobats, Amish people who still drove a horse and buggy, women with stretched necks, bound feet, or corseted waists.

"Dad," I said. "I want to travel."

He sank to the edge of the bed and touched Granny's forehead. "Sure, Caye," he said. "Where do you want to go? You know summer's not the best time since the gardens need tending, but we could go somewhere this fall."

"Not with the family," I said, swallowing hard. "I love you guys, but I'm not a kid anymore, Dad."

His eyes skittered over my torn dress, and he stiffened. "I see."

"I want to see and do more than I can in this valley," I said. "Just for a few years."

"I'll talk to the collective."

"Okay," I said. "Thanks, Dad. But it's really not up to them anymore."

"Just be careful."

"I will," I said. "We will. I want to take my collective."

"Malik?"

"And Efrain," I said, feeling shy suddenly. I picked up Granny's hand and closed my fingers around hers. "And his brothers."

Before Dad could answer, Granny's eyes flew open. She blinked at us blindly for a second.

"Granny," I said. "You're awake."

"How did you get up here?" she asked, pushing herself up on her elbows.

My familiar stirred, going on alert, as if it didn't know her. I shushed it with calming magic and gripped Granny's hand. "We flew," I said. "I'm so glad you're awake. What happened? How did you get here? I went to your house and you were gone."

She narrowed her eyes, studying us for a minute. I'd never seen that look in her eyes, like she was calculating something. Granny's spaciness could be frustrating. Sometimes she blurted out the wrong things or changed topic with no warning in the middle of a conversation. But she never looked like that.

"Gran," I said. "Why are you looking at us like that?"

"Like what?" She jerked upright as if she'd been caught in a daydream.

"I don't know," I said. "Sorry. Let's get you out of here."

"Yes, let's," she said, her face brightening. "Will you carry me out? Gosh, this body is a dump. It barely works."

That wasn't something Granny Golden would say.

Dad frowned, patting his own familiar, a mink that was baring its teeth. "Did you hit your head?"

She laughed, a weird, high-pitched laugh that I'd never heard before. "Of course not," she said, swatting his arm in a way that was almost flirtatious.

Which was extra creepy, since she was his mom.

"I'll carry you down," he said, but he was still looking at her suspiciously.

"No, I want you to do it, dear," she said, her hand closing around my arm with unusual strength.

"What a strong grip you've developed," I said. "But I don't really think I can lift you."

"Your magic can, though," she said, sliding her arm around my shoulder. I tried not to wrinkle my nose—it was obvious she hadn't bathed since coming here. I used some more air magic to help lift her from the bed. Dad went to the window, watching warily as I approached carrying Granny. He slipped out in front of me and hovered there, waiting to catch her if she slipped. I was halfway out when the realization of what was wrong hit me like a magical fireball.

"Gran," I gasped. "You have magic."

She lurched forward, yanking me off the ledge and out the window.

Chapter Twenty-Six

Cayenne

Panic explode inside me. At the same moment, a bird hurled itself at us. I hit the wall, my head spinning with pain. For a second, I couldn't see anything. I was crushed, sliding, hands gripping me in strange places. When my head cleared, I found myself pinned to the wall by Efrain's body. He was gripping the window ledge above, using his knees to hold me up and pin me against the wall. Dad was lowering himself to the ground with Granny, assisted by some of the other witches' air magic.

"I'd like this a lot more if you were naked, too," Efrain said, his voice strained.

"We have an audience."

"Perfect opportunity for me to show off."

"Get off me," I said, pushing him away.

"Isn't that what the rest of the collective is for?" he said, releasing me from the grip of his knees. "Or do we all participate at the same time? I'm cool either way."

"There's a lot more to it than that," I said, lowering myself toward the ground with my air magic.

"I'm here to learn," he called, still hanging from the window.

A minute later, he joined us in bird form. I found Oral on the ground, along with my aunt Willow, who they knew as Dr. Golden. Oral and Malik both stepped forward to embrace me at the same time.

They paused, though, when a commotion started where Dad had set down. "You're not my mother," he said. "Who are you? And where's my mother?"

"Fine, I'm not that old hag," Granny said, struggling to pick herself up from the ground where Dad had lain her. "Like I'd want to keep this slow old thing. You can have it back."

Dad grabbed her shoulders. "Where is my mother?"

"She's gone," she said, pulling away. "Cayenne told me she was sick, so I went out there to that hut, and she was breathing her last breath. I only just got there in time to save her body for a few days."

"You're using her body? Why?"

"So I could do the job that this fool couldn't," she said, pointing a crooked finger at Efrain. "I told you to get my daughter, not this witch. Do I have to do everything myself?"

"I thought she was your daughter," Efrain said, putting an arm over my shoulders.

"You got the wrong girl, bird-brain," she said. "I have to be in three places at once to get my job done. I just borrowed this body. You're welcome to have it back."

"You're a body snatcher?" Efrain asked.

"I just borrow the ones not being used anymore," she said. "I never hurt anyone."

"Yvonne," Dad said, his eyes narrowing. "If you hurt my mother, so help me…"

I exchanged a glance with Malik. Yvonne might be annoying, the way she was always trying to look like a teenager and get in our business. I'd never known her to want to be old.

"She was already gone," Yvonne—in Granny's body—wailed.

"If we find out otherwise, you'll be banished from the coven," Dad said to Yvonne. "Permanently."

As her words sunk in, I sagged against Malik. Granny Golden was gone. I hadn't even gotten a chance to say goodbye. All the time I'd been looking for her, and she'd been dead all along. My throat tightened as Malik's strong, familiar embrace took me in.

"Well, I think I can speak for the entire shifter valley when I say, stay the hell out," Efrain said. "We don't welcome body-snatchers. That's not how we shift into animal form."

"If you ever show up there as a mouse, expect to be eaten," Oral said.

"Wait," I said, pulling away from Malik and facing the coven. "I don't think she's lying. Yvonne wants to be younger, not older. And there's no reason for all this hatred between the valleys. I'm upset about my granny, too, but Yvonne's not to blame. And we don't have to have all these divisions."

"She tried to force you to marry that wolf," Oral said.

"Actually, Efrain did," I reminded him. "And she wasn't trying to do anything to me. He got the wrong person. I love this valley, and after seeing how other people live, I know I want to raise my kids in peace, the way my parents raised me. But I want them to know people who aren't just like them, too. All kinds of people."

"We have many supernaturals in our valley," Mom said. "Hell, only one of your fathers is a warlock."

"But why do we pick and choose which people belong? Until the other day, I'd never even talked to a shifter except in passing. And why is one kind of shifting okay and another isn't? She didn't hurt anyone, and I watched you two murder wolves." I glared at Oral, who dropped his gaze, and Efrain, who frowned.

"Thank you," Yvonne said.

"I'm not doing this for you," I said, my fist tightening. "Get out of my granny's body right now. It's a sacrilege to use her dead body for your own purposes."

"Fine, fine," she said, lowering herself to the ground. She closed her eyes, and after a moment, her body went limp.

I ran to her and knelt beside her. Yvonne had kept her body alive, and now that she was gone, Granny was truly gone.

A tear slipped from my eye and fell onto her withered other hand. "I love you, Granny," I whispered. "I'm going to make you proud."

*

As the coven returned to our valley to prepare for Granny's burial, I asked Malik to join me as we followed the shifters back to Nelson's house. He wanted to know what was going on, but I didn't want to explain until we were all together.

When we reached Nelson's, the guys hesitated. "He's not in good shape," Efrain said, frowning at Malik as if he were an intruder.

I took Malik's hand. "I need to see him. We all do. Together."

When we stepped into the house, Malik stiffened. "Cayenne," he said quietly. "This is a magical dead space."

So, they'd picked up the stupid rock I'd thrown. It was okay here, protecting his house, but if they ever put it on me again, I really would curse them.

"I know," I said. "They won't hurt us. They know better."

"That's some exercise in trust," he muttered as we headed for the stairs. "I'm surprised you'd come in here after what they did."

"Since when are you so suspicious?" I teased.

Efrain opened the door to Nelson's bedroom, and Oral stepped in. "We brought visitors," he said. "Cayenne."

Nelson's voice was sharp. "Why'd you bring her here? I don't want her to see me like this."

"It's okay," I said, dropping Malik's hand and approaching the bed. I sat beside Nelson, who looked grey and grim. "I'm sorry. I couldn't wait to see you again."

He turned his face away, his jaw tight.

"I guess I owe you some introductions," I said, standing and pulling my dress together at the top. "Malik, I found my collective."

"That was fast."

I shrugged. "When you know, you know."

His forehead creased into a frown. "Does that mean you don't know about me? Because it's been years…"

"I know about you," I said, squeezing his hand. "I didn't know before, because you were only part of it. Now that I found the rest, I'm sure about you, too. I'm sure about all of you, as a whole."

"They're…shifters?"

"Yep," I said, nodding at the others.

"I guess you inherited your love of variety from your mom," he said.

Mom was one of the few witches who had married men from outside the coven, but it went back further than that.

205

"Not Mom," I said. "Granny Golden. She's the person who taught me what love really means. She was the first in our coven to marry someone who wasn't a warlock."

"Does this mean you want us for your collective for more than one day?" Oral asked, grinning.

My face warmed at the memory of what a day that had been. "Yes," I said.

"Nelson's hurt real bad," Oral said, his smile fading.

"I wouldn't add anything," Nelson said, his eyes finding mine. "I can't."

"That doesn't matter," I said, leaning down to smooth his forehead. I pressed a gentle kiss on his lips. "I love you for who you are, not how long your arms are. I'll be here to nurse you back to health for as long as you'll have me."

"Well," Malik said. "Life's about to get interesting in our house."

I grinned at him. "Did you expect anything less?"

"No," he said. "I'm glad you didn't ditch me when you found these men."

"I would never," I said, standing on tiptoes to give him a quick kiss. "I always knew I'd marry you one day. I just didn't know who else would be part of our family. But before we settle down, I want to travel, see the world, and go on grand adventures like Granny Golden."

Malik smiled down at me. "Life with you is always an adventure."

I took one of his hands and one of Oral's, and I smiled down at Nelson. "And we're just getting started."

From the Author

Thank you for reading *Twisted!* I hope you enjoyed little glimpses of *The Three Little Pigs* and *Little Red Riding Hood* as well as the original aspects of the story. If you enjoyed the mash-up style of these two tales, make sure to look for the second book in the series, *Caged,* where *Rapunzel* melds with *Jack and the Beanstalk.* It's available now on Amazon in ebook and paperback format.

This story fits into a larger world of fairytales and Norse mythology that encompasses most of my writing. You can explore those worlds and spot familiar faces in other stories, including <u>Girl Among Wolves Trilogy</u> (where you'll meet that handsome werewolf alpha who received Cayenne at the eclipse) and <u>Winslow Witch Chronicles</u> (where you'll travel back to the 80's when the Big Bad Warlock was reaping havoc on the witch community).

www.ingramcontent.com/pod-product-compliance
Lightning Source LLC
Chambersburg PA
CBHW020950180626
46814CB00003B/1027